THE 5 MINUTE
MINUTE
BRAIN WORKOUT

foR KiDS

365 Amazing, Fabulous, and Fun Word Puzzles

KIM CHAMBERLAIN
ILLUSTRATIONS BY JON CHAMBERLAIN

Sky Pony Press
New York

Sky Pony Press books may be purchased in bulk at special discounts for sales promotion, corporate gifts, fund-raising, or educational purposes. Special editions can also be created to specifications. For details, contact the Special Sales Department, Sky Pony Press, 307 West 36th Street, 11th Floor, New York, NY 10018 or info@ skyhorsepublishing.com.

Sky Pony® is a registered trademark of Skyhorse Publishing, Inc.®, a Delaware corporation.

Visit our website at www.skyponypress.com.

10 9 8 7 6 5 4 3 2 1

Manufactured in China, July 2015
This product conforms to CPSIA 2008

Library of Congress Cataloging-in-Publication Data is available on file.

Cover design by Gretchen Schuler
Cover illustration credit Jon Chamberlain and Thinkstock

Print ISBN: 978-1-63450-159-0

Contents

Introduction for Children

Hello, and welcome to *The Five-Minute Brain Workout for Kids*! This is a book full of short, fun games and puzzles that will keep your brain active and help it develop.

Spending a few minutes each day doing these exercises can help you in many ways. These puzzles and games can:

- help you learn new words;
- help you with spelling;
- help your brain work a bit faster;
- help you with problem solving;
- help you with concentration skills;
- let you have fun, either on your own or with friends or parents;
- help you develop a love of words;
- help you set goals and challenges, for example by setting a timer or by aiming to get to Level 10.

There are 365 games and puzzles in this book, which means you have enough for a year's worth of brain workout. So let's get started. . . .

Introduction for Parents

What are the benefits of word games and puzzles?

Adults and children alike love word puzzles. Not only can the puzzles bring hours of fun and entertainment, but they can also offer a number of educational and personal benefits. These include:

- consolidating and increasing vocabulary;
- helping with the spelling of known and new words;
- developing the discipline to solve the puzzles;
- developing the creativity to complete the games;
- improving thinking speed;
- fostering problem solving skills;
- developing concentration skills;
- encouraging goal setting, for example aiming to work through to Level 10;
- gaining a sense of achievement as they complete the games and puzzles and work through the levels;
- setting personal challenges, for example completing the puzzles within a specific time frame;
- allowing for a fun and healthy sense of competition with others and
- encouraging a love of words and language by seeing words in an enjoyable and interesting way.

Also, the games and puzzles can be done jointly with family, with friends, in class with a teacher, and in other group situations.

In addition, the book is fairly easy to carry around and use. You don't need any special equipment or technology, and, in fact, it gives children a break from being connected to a device.

The concepts in this book include:

- Acronyms
- Alliteration
- Alphabet; alphabetical order; reverse alphabetical order
- Anagrams; rearranging letters, words, and sentences
- Compound words
- Concentration
- Creativity
- Definitions
- Homophones and homonyms
- Matching words—antonyms, synonyms, opposites, pairs
- Parts of speech—nouns, pronouns, verbs, adverbs, adjectives, comparative, superlative
- Patterns
- Problem solving
- Rhyming words
- Silent letters
- Spelling
- Syllables
- Vocabulary
- Word structure—vowels and consonants; capitals and lower case; letter differentiation; letter shapes
- Word categories

How the Book Is Laid Out

Games & Puzzles

There are 365 exercises in this book, enough for one puzzle per day. The exercises are made up of thirty-seven different types of word games and puzzles, spaced evenly throughout the book. Thirty-six types have ten exercises, while the thirty-seventh has five exercises.

Levels

There are ten levels, Level 1 to Level 10. The exercises usually get harder as you go through the book. This means that the Level 10 games and puzzles will usually be more difficult than the ones before.

The difference between a game and a puzzle

A puzzle has a specific answer, for example a Word Sudoku, while a game will have a number of suitable answers, for example, "Think of a word that has two syllables and starts with 'V.'" This means you can develop your creativity by doing each game more than once and getting different answers. About two-thirds of the exercises are puzzles and about one third are games.

Variety

There are many of types of exercises (thirty-seven to be exact) that will make your brain work in different ways and keep it alert.

Bonus

Try the three bonus puzzles at the end.

Answers

You will find the answers at the back of the book. The puzzles have specific answers, while the games have examples of suitable answers.

How to Use This Book

First of all, feel free to use the book in any way you like. There is no right or wrong way to use it.

A suggested way is to start at the beginning and do all the Level 1 games and puzzles—one a day—through all the levels until you reach Level 10. Or, you may like to choose one type of game or puzzle and work through all ten levels, before going back to a new puzzle and doing the same.

As many of the exercises will be new to you, it's a good idea to take time to read the instructions so that you can use the five minutes for each game or puzzle well.

The games and puzzles will probably take you different amounts of time. Some may not take the full five minutes, while some may take you slightly longer. That's okay.

If you are not sure how to tackle a game or puzzle, look at the answer in the back and work out how it's done. Then you'll know how to do the next one.

As well as a way to exercise your brain, the games and puzzles can be used to challenge yourself, or simply to have fun. Or you can add a competitive element by using a timer or doing them with others.

A note from the illustrator and author, husband and wife team Jon and Kim:

We chose to use a lizard for many of the illustrations because we have a pet lizard at home. He is a blue-tongued lizard called Ra. He is friendly, tame, and very happy to be held. He has no idea that he is the model for the drawings!

Level 1

Word Line 1

Start at the letter in the circle and draw a continuous line right, left, up, or down (though not diagonally) to find the letters in the saying. The punctuation marks are not included.

"Time's fun when you're having flies."
Kermit the Frog

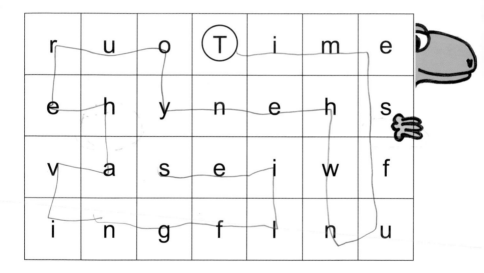

Umbrella Words 1

These umbrellas have letters on them. With the umbrella closed you can only see two letters. Use your imagination to work out words that might be written on the umbrella when it is open. The word has to contain these two letters in this order, but it can be as long or short as you like, and the letters can appear anywhere in the word. The first one has been done for you.

Train Words 1

Can you find the three-letter names of animals hidden in the train cars? Put a circle around them.

~~ram~~   ~~cat~~   ~~bat~~   ~~yak~~   ~~rat~~   ~~ape~~

Anagrams 1

Work out the anagrams below, then draw a line between the words that are opposites. The first one has been done for you.

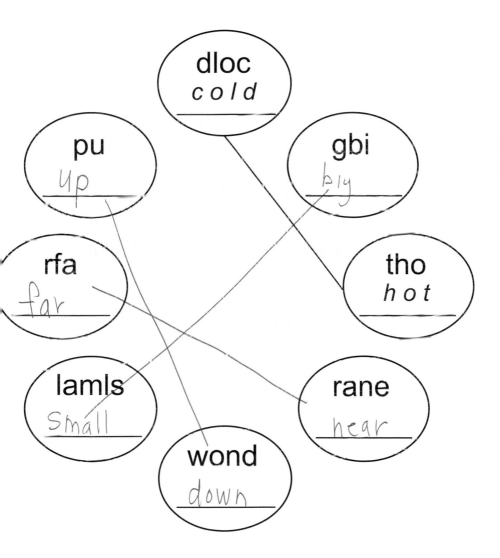

Alphabet Teasers 1

Choose words that fit into the grid using the letters given.

One has been done for you.

Begins with	Animal	Place	Boy's name
T	Tiger	Topeka	Tom
S	Sheep	Siam	Steven
P	Porcupine	Paris	Peter
L	Llama	Long Island	Len

Fishing 1

Fish for the right letters to make words that solve the clues.

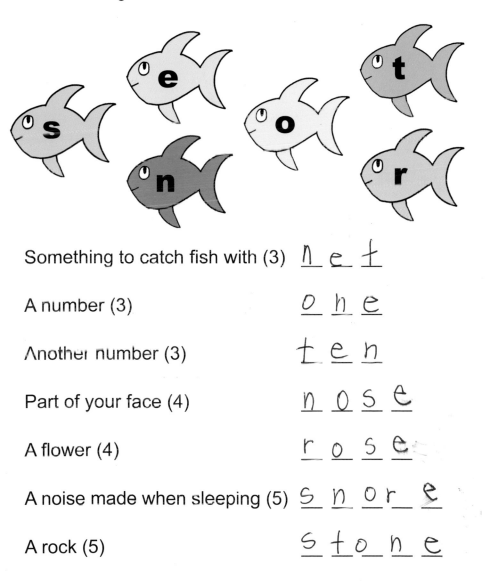

Something to catch fish with (3)   n e t

A number (3)   o n e

Another number (3)   t e n

Part of your face (4)   n o s e

A flower (4)   r o s e

A noise made when sleeping (5)   s n o r e

A rock (5)   s t o n e

Mini Word Sudoku 1

Write a letter from the four-letter word "read" in each square so that each column, row, and mini-grid contains all the letters from the word.

r		e	
		d	
	r	a	
a			d

Alphabet 1

Cross out the letters that are in the grid twice. Then rearrange the letters that are left to spell two words that are opposites.

Answer:

Time to Rhyme 1

Write down five words, one in each petal, that rhyme with the word in the center.

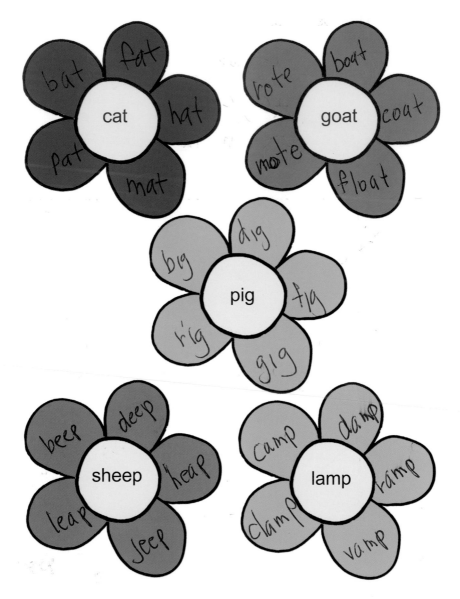

The Big X Word Search 1

The words to find are in pairs. You will find each pair of words in the shape of an X.

The first one has been done for you: FUNNY- BENDY

Can you find:
SCARY - BLACK ✓
CLEAN - GREEN ✓
JOLLY - SILLY ✓
CRISP - WHITE ✓

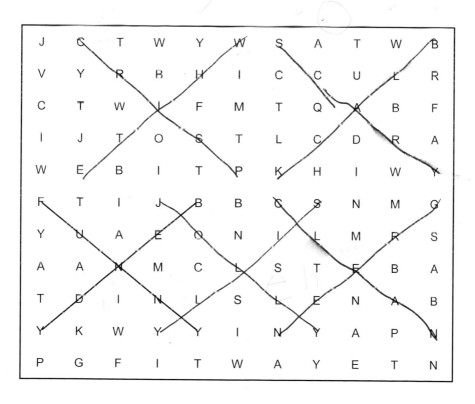

The Word Store 1

The Word Store is a special place that sells different kinds of words. Today we are going shopping for **adjectives** (describing words). Wherever there is a space in the story, write in an adjective that starts with the letter given. It's a good idea to read through the story first to get a feel for what you may want to write. If you write in pencil, you can do it more than once and make the story different each time.

Alice was an a _attractive_ girl who had a very b _right_ brother called Callum. Alice wanted a c _alico_ cat, but Callum preferred a d _aring_ dog, and they couldn't agree.

"Why don't we get an e _nergetic_ bird?" asked Mom.

"Or a f _urry_ rabbit instead?"

"No," said Callum, "birds are g _rabby_ !"

"But a h _ungry_ rabbit would be okay," said Alice. "Perhaps we could get it an i _deal_ hutch to live in."

"Okay," said Callum, "as long as it's a j _olly_ rabbit."

"Great," said Mom. "We'll go the pet shop tomorrow."

Letters 1

Color the squares with **consonants** in **brown**.
Color the squares with **vowels** in **yellow**.
Then work out what the picture is.

H	Q	G	S	D	C	F	P	P	C
J	F	L	P	J	G	B	J	S	D
B	S	A	I	O	U	E	I	H	L
P	C	U	B	C	S	L	A	L	B
Q	E	O	A	I	O	A	U	E	F
F	A	U	I	E	E	A	O	I	C
G	O	E	A	U	O	O	U	A	D
S	U	A	U	E	A	I	I	O	S
D	E	I	O	I	E	A	U	E	F
L	H	B	S	F	H	J	F	Q	L

Words and Sounds 1

Homophones are words that are spelled and pronounced the same, but have different meanings. The story below contains two words that are pronounced the same, though only one of them has the right meaning in the sentence. Cross off the wrong one.

Joy goes for a walk

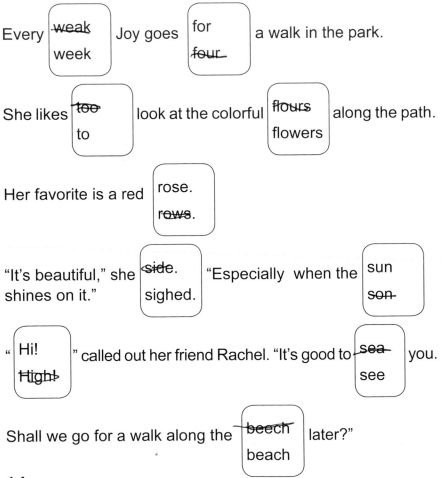

Every ~~weak~~ / week Joy goes for / ~~four~~ a walk in the park.

She likes ~~too~~ / to look at the colorful ~~flours~~ / flowers along the path.

Her favorite is a red rose. / ~~rows.~~

"It's beautiful," she ~~side.~~ / sighed. "Especially when the sun / ~~son~~ shines on it."

" Hi! / ~~Hight~~ " called out her friend Rachel. "It's good to ~~sea~~ / see you.

Shall we go for a walk along the ~~beech~~ / beach later?"

14

Synonyms 1

A synonym is a word that means exactly or nearly the same as another word; for example, "sad" and "unhappy" are synonyms. Find the pairs of synonyms and draw a line connecting the two.

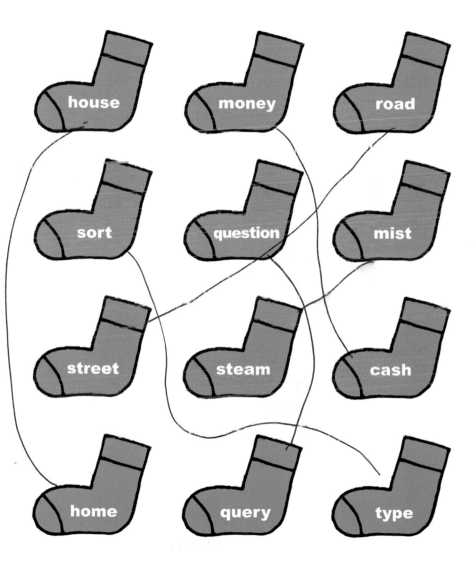

Acronyms 1

Acronyms are words formed from the initial letters of other words. For example, **ASPS** could stand for "American Society Protecting Snakes."

Work out what the acronyms could stand for, then make up one of your own at the end.

Theme: ANIMALS

ASPS — American Society Protecting Snakes

SoLL — Society of Leaping Lizards

PADO — Pan American Dog Owners

BOO — Bureau of Octopus Owners

Definitions 1

Choose the correct definition for each word.

Imaginary	1) A photograph 2) Witchcraft 3) Not real *(circled)*
Albino	1) The white of an egg 2) Person with white skin and hair, and pink eyes *(circled)* 3) The Roman name for Britain
Asterisk	1) A plant 2) Warrior with great power 3) A star-shaped symbol *(circled)*
Narrator	1) Person who tells a story *(circled)* 2) The county where someone is born 3) A swimmer
Floppy	1) Having big ears 2) Soft and bendy *(circled)* 3) Fancy

Leaping Lizard 1

The words of a sentence have been jumbled up and placed onto rocks. The lizard is leaping from the rock with the first word, to the one with the second word. Work out which order the words go in, and draw a line to show the lizard which way to jump. The first one has been done for you.

You can write the sentence at the bottom.

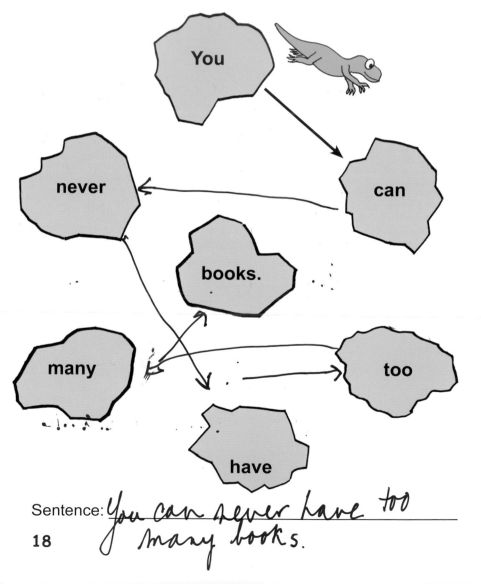

Sentence: *You can never have too many books.*

Syllables 1

Add a letter or letters to the ones already given to make words that are 1, 2, and 3 syllables long.
The first one has been done for you.
Note that the sound of the vowel may change, for example, "low" and "logic." That's okay.

	1 syllable	2 syllables	3 syllables
Lo	Low	Logic	Lollipop
Car	Carp	Carpet	Carpentar
Ban	Band	Bandage	Banana
Me	Met	Meatball	Metallic

Compound Words 1

A compound word is formed when two words join together to become a new word; for example, softball, teapot, and armchair.

Draw lines between the two parts of the compound words.

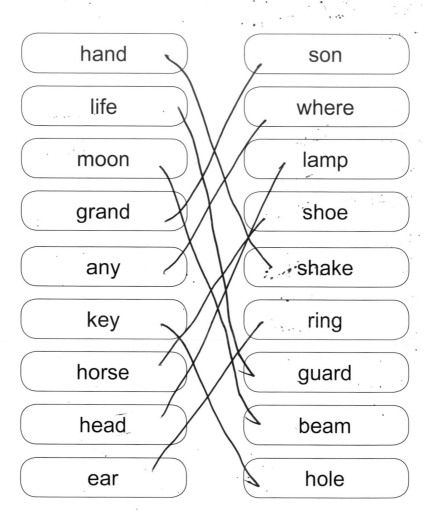

hand	son
life	where
moon	lamp
grand	shoe
any	shake
key	ring
horse	guard
head	beam
ear	hole

Continuous Words 1

This is a list of words joined together with the word spaces taken out. How many can you find?

Topic: VEGETABLES

outs *pepper* *an* *bean* *kin* *be* *ump* *pumpkin*
outs

cornasparagusspinachcucumberradishb
roccolicauliflowerturnippeascabbagecele
rylettucebeetroottomatopotatoonioncarrotp
umpkinbeanpeppersprouts *pep* *pump*

corn	cucumber	broccoli	peas
as		colic	pea
asparagus	rad radish	cauliflower	cabbage
spin	dish	flow	bag
in	sprouts	turn	age
spinach	bee	hip	cab
celery	beet	turnip	on
lettuce	root	top	onion
let	otto	pot	car
	to	potato	rot
	Tom	toon	carrot
	mat		
	at		

Speed Words 1

Choose words that fit the description. Use words that don't start with a capital letter, and use a different word for each question.

Choose a word that:

yule   *yike*
         yelp

1	Starts with Y and has 4 letters	yank your year yard yawn yell
2	Has 5 letters and starts and ends with T	table teach talks tacky taffy tames tapes tarps taffy
3	Contains 2 O's together	book coo coop broom boo cool coot bloom cook coon boom doon
4	Has 2 L's and ends in Y	belly jolly holly rally jelly dolly lolly tally folly molly
5	Has 2 syllables and starts with V	very valid vermouth vermeer value valor velour visor voicebox

tales
tails

② takes tans tars tales taste taxes

22

Concentration 1

Either underline or put a circle around the nouns in the passage (not proper nouns, which have a capital letter, or pronouns, which are words like "I", "you," or "he").

Wilma Gets It Wrong

Wilma is a kind and mischievous witch who lives in the woods. She has a broomstick and a black cat and likes to play tricks on people.

One Saturday she felt bored and decided to fly into the next wood where she saw a family eating a picnic.

"I see a young boy being naughty," she said to herself. "I will turn him into a big brown toad to teach him a lesson!"

However, the young boy liked being a toad. He jumped onto the sandwiches and into the bowl of cream and then ate the strawberries.

"Hmm," thought Wilma, "this hasn't worked. I will have to change him back."

23

Vocabulary 1

Fit the three-letter words into the correct spaces in the larger words.

ANT   AND   ART   IMP   ILL   EBB

P I M P LE

P A N D A

P E B B LE

P I L L OW

P A N T HER

P A R T NER

Change a Letter 1

Change one letter in the word so it fits the definition.
The first one has been done for you.

Word	Definition	New word
PEAR	Furry animal	BEAR
PEAR	Expensive	DEAR
PEAR	Feeling scared	FEAR
PINE	A drink	WINE
PINE	A color	PINK
PINE	Sheet of glass	PANE
PEST	Relax	REST
PEST	Some time ago	PAST
PEST	Bird's shelter	NEST

Hat Words 1

Fill in the rows with words of your choice, starting with a one-letter word and ending with an eight-letter word. Try not to use plurals.

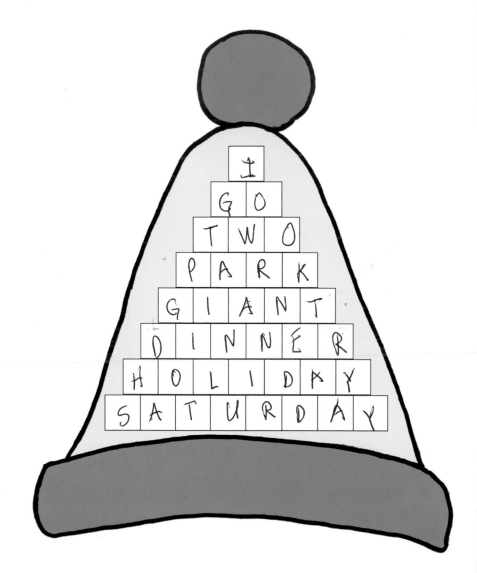

Categories 1

The list contains words that fall into two categories: colors and tastes.

Write the words into the correct category in the balloons.

beige   bitter   crimson   indigo   acidic   salty

mild   bronze   spicy   sour   jade   russet

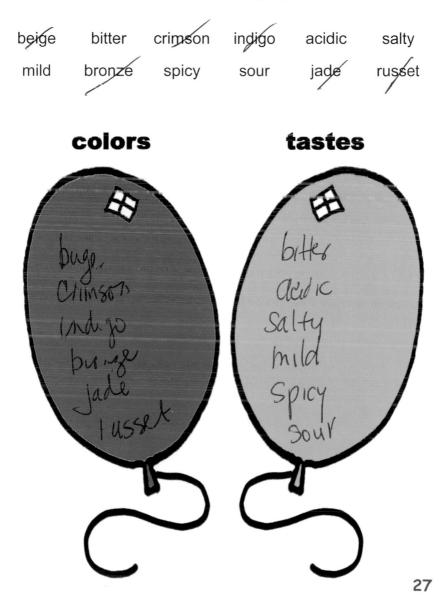

colors

bige,
Crimson
indigo
bunge
jade
I usset

tastes

bitter
acidic
salty
mild
spicy
sour

Gridword 1

Place the words so they fit in the grid. The first word has been filled in for you.

LOYAL
TIRED
YODEL
HONEY
NERVY
HOTEL

H	O	N	E	Y
O		E		O
T	I	R	E	D
E		V		E
L	O	Y	A	L

Lizard in a Cave 1

Each cave has an anagram of an creature.
Today the lizard wants to go in the cave that has another **reptile**. Solve the anagrams and write the words beneath the caves, then color in or put a circle around the cave the lizard would like to go in. The first anagram has been done for you.

E R O H S

horse

E K S N A

snake

G E R I T

tiger

E H E S P

sheep

S O M E O

moose

29

How Many 1

How many words can you think of that <u>only</u> contain one vowel, the letter **A**? The letter A can be anywhere in the word.
Aim for the number stated in each column, though you can do more if you like.
A couple have been done for you.

Words that contain the letter **A**		
1 A Aim for 10	2 A's Aim for 2	3 or more A's Aim for 1
cat Jack acid able actual add aerial after agree hear aisle	alarm algae aggravate gravitate	Calamari ~~pastram~~

Change and Rhyme 1

Change one letter in both words in the pair so that they rhyme.
For example LIFT & WIRE becomes LIFE & WIFE.
There may be more than one solution.

NEAT & RENT
S   S

BEE   KNEE
BET & KNEW

Q Crosswords 1

A straightforward crossword in the shape of a Q.

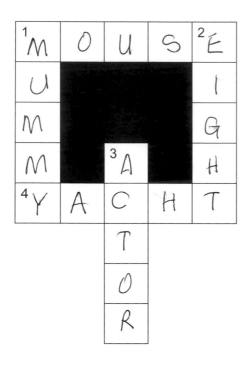

ACROSS
1. A creature that squeaks
4. It sails on water

DOWN
1. Person wrapped in bandages
2. Fourteen plus six, minus twelve
3. Male person in a play

Wheel Words 1

Work out what the word in each wheel reads. The letters go in a clockwise direction, and the word can start anywhere in the wheel.

Topic: ANIMALS

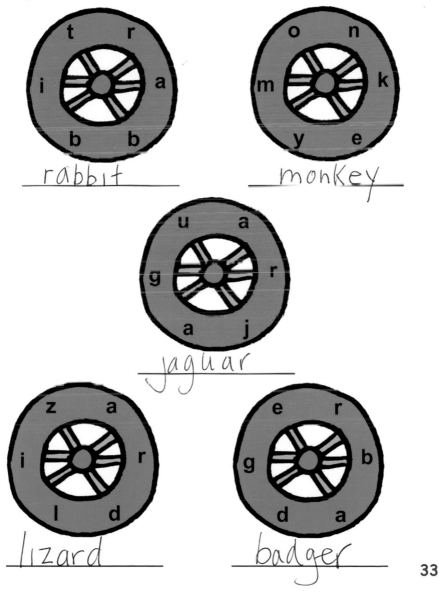

rabbit

monkey

jaguar

lizard

badger

Weird & Wonderful Words 1

Make a new compound word by choosing a word from each column and joining them together.
Write a description of what this new word means, and then write a sentence showing how it's used.
An example has been given for you.

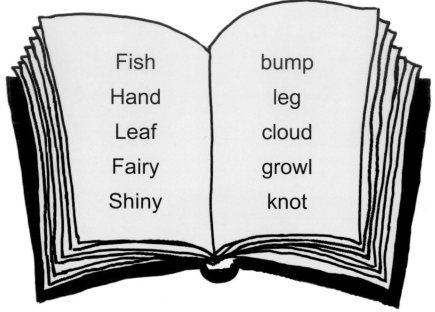

Fish — bump
Hand — leg
Leaf — cloud
Fairy — growl
Shiny — knot

EXAMPLE
WORD: **Fishcloud**
DESCRIPTION: A small cloud-shaped water container with holes, that goes over a fish tank. As you pour water in, it looks like rain so the fish think they are in open water.
SENTENCE: On hot sunny days we use the fishcloud so that the fish feel cooler and think they are in a pond.

Now it's your turn!
WORD: handknot
DESCRIPTION: a series of knots, consisting of 5 adjacent knots, used to hold keys
SENTENCE: He kept his keys on a handknot for easy access

Remove a Letter 1

Take one letter out of each word, so that the words make a real sentence.
For example, if you take one letter out of each of these words, PIT HIS AN WHEN, it becomes IT IS A HEN.

THEY COAT SEAT ONE

THEN MOAT

AEIOU1

The vowels A E I O U are missing from the following words. Work out which vowel goes in which word, but check carefully before you write them in!
Cross off the vowels as you use them.

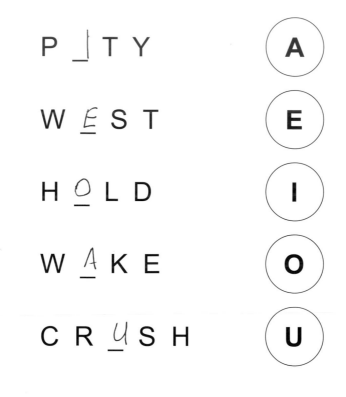

P I T Y   **A**

W E S T   **E**

H O L D   **I**

W A K E   **O**

C R U S H   **U**

Skillful Sentences 1

Can you write a sentence—or sentences—with at least four words, where all the words start with the letter S?

Stop saying silly
sentences, Sara

In the Middle 1

Work out what word goes in the middle. The first one has been done for you

March	*April*	May
Beginning	middle	End
Egg	Chick	Hen
Cold	Warm	Hot
Two	four	Six
Good	better	Best
Black	gray	White
Bronze	silver	Gold

Level 2

Word Line 2

Start at the letter in the circle and draw a continuous line right, left, up, or down (though not diagonally) to find the letters in the saying. The punctuation marks are not included.

"All you need is faith, hope, and pixie dust!"
Peter Pan

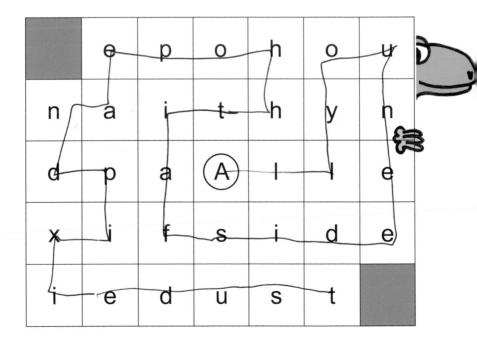

Umbrella Words 2

These umbrellas have letters on them. With the umbrella closed you can only see two letters. Work out words that might be written on the umbrella when it is open. The word has to contain these two letters in this order, but it can be as long or short as you like, and the letters can appear anywhere in the word. See if you can find different ways to include the letters in a word.

g r — grate — gray — aggrevate

s h — hush — shallow — marshmallw

e e — eek! — breen — seem

b a — abba — bait — baby

Train Words 2

Can you find the three-letter names of parts of the body hidden in the train cars? Put a circle around them.

~~rib~~   ~~ear~~   ~~eye~~   ~~arm~~   ~~lip~~   leg

Anagrams 2

Work out the anagrams, then draw a line between the words that are opposites.

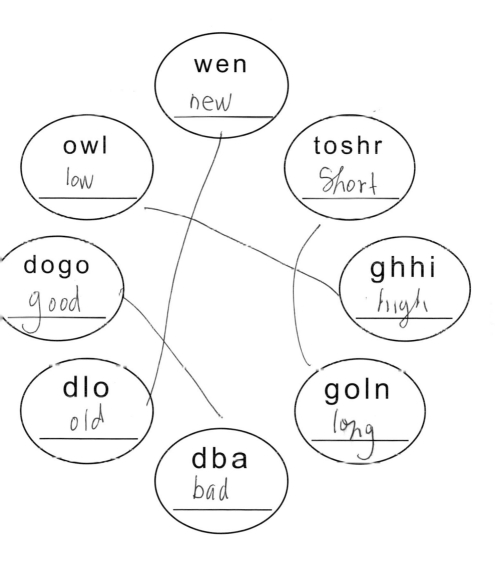

wen
new

owl
low

toshr
Short

dogo
good

ghhi
high

dlo
old

goln
long

dba
bad

Alphabet Teasers 2

Choose words that fit into the grid using the letters given.

Begins with	Food	Color	Girl's name
G	green beans	green	Gloria
R	raisins	red	Rita
B	beets	blue	Betty
P	pizza	pink	Patricia

Fishing 2

Fish for the right letters to make words that solve the clues.

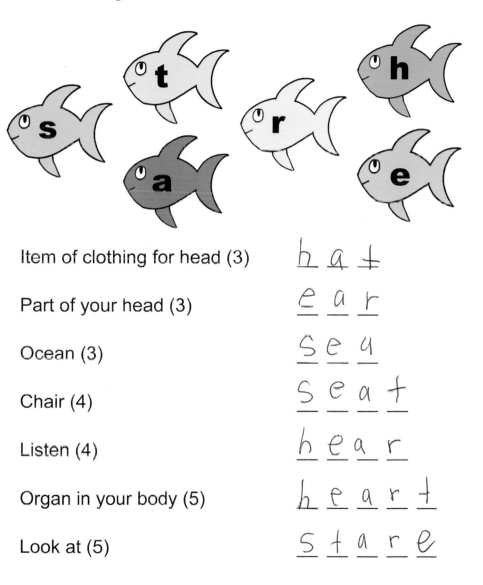

Item of clothing for head (3)   h a t

Part of your head (3)   e a r

Ocean (3)   s e a

Chair (4)   s e a t

Listen (4)   h e a r

Organ in your body (5)   h e a r t

Look at (5)   s t a r e

Mini Word Sudoku 2

Write a letter from the four-letter word **"word"** in each square so that each column, row, and mini-grid contains all the letters from the word.

d	o	r	w
w	d	o	r
r	w	d	o
o	r	w	d

Alphabet 2

Work out which letters of the alphabet are missing, then rearrange them to make the name of a color.

f	i	z	r	k
s	q	i	a	t
m	y	a	x	n
v	e	m	p	g
h	f	y	t	o
w	o	p	j	d

Missing letters

b	e	l	

Rearrange letters to make the name of a color: __ __ __ __

Time to Rhyme 2

Write down five words, one in each petal, that rhyme with the word in the center.

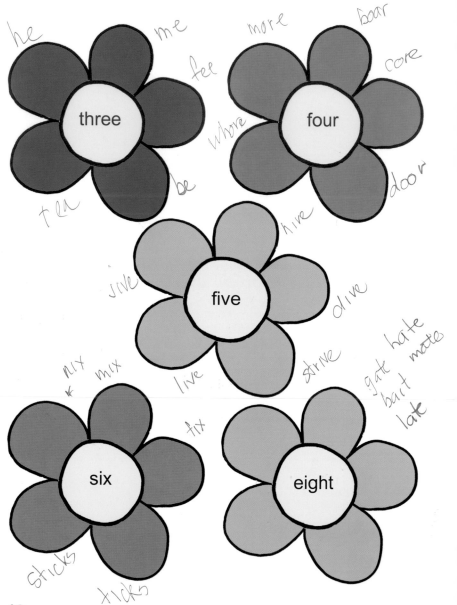

three
- he
- me
- fee
- whore
- be
- tea

four
- more
- boar
- core
- door

five
- hire
- dive
- strive
- live
- jive

six
- nix
- mix
- fix
- sticks
- ticks

eight
- gate
- hate
- mate
- bait
- late

The Big X Word Search 2

The words to find are in pairs. You will find each pair of words in the shape of an X.

Can you find:
MISTY - DUSTY
BRIEF - QUICK
HUSKY - RASPY
FANCY - DANDY
AGILE - BRISK

The Word Store 2

The Word Store is a special place that sells different kinds of words. Today we are going shopping for **adjectives** (describing words). Wherever there is a space in the story, write in an adjective that starts with the letter given. It's a good idea to read through the story first to get a feel for what you may want to write. If you write in pencil, you can do the puzzle more than once and make the story different each time.

The Word Store

Norman was very n_osey_

and sometimes his mom wished

he was o_verly cautious_.

His sister Pauline was very

p_oised_ and usually

q_uiet_. One day Norman was being

more r_ough_ than ever and his mom

shouted, "Stop being s_tupid_! I'm too

t_ired_ to cope with it."

Norman looked u_pset_ so his dad said,

"We all need to do something w_onderful_!

Let's go for a drive, buy some y_ellow_ ice

cream, and then go to the beach."

50

Letters 2

Color the squares with **consonants** in **green**.
Color the squares with **vowels** in **gray**.
Then work out what the picture is.

d	j	c	s	y	v	c	r	d	g
v	b	p	f	g	b	y	h	p	r
h	a	i	o	r	f	u	o	i	j
c	o	e	i	s	g	e	a	u	h
b	u	a	e	j	y	a	i	e	v
s	d	y	f	r	d	g	f	b	s
v	p	c	h	v	h	s	d	c	g
j	c	o	e	a	o	i	u	p	r
s	b	u	i	u	e	a	o	b	j
c	r	v	g	p	y	j	h	d	p

Words and Sounds 2

Homophones are words that are spelled and pronounced the same, but have different meanings.

The story below contains two words that are pronounced the same, though only one of them has the right meaning in the sentence. Cross off the wrong one.

Haunted house

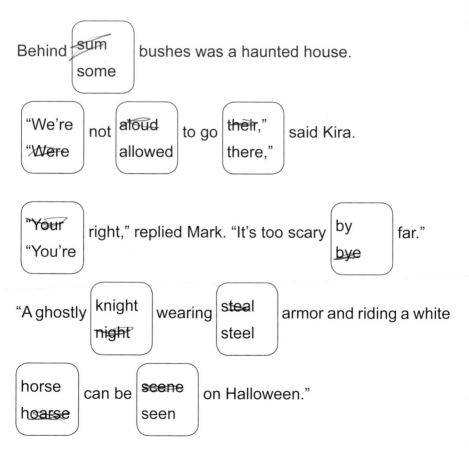

Behind ~~sum~~ / some bushes was a haunted house.

"We're / ~~Were~~ not ~~aloud~~ / allowed to go ~~their~~ / there," said Kira.

"~~Your~~ / You're right," replied Mark. "It's too scary by / ~~bye~~ far."

"A ghostly knight / ~~night~~ wearing ~~steal~~ / steel armor and riding a white

horse / ~~hoarse~~ can be ~~scene~~ / seen on Halloween."

52

Synonyms 2

A synonym is a word that means exactly or nearly the same as another word; for example "sad" and "unhappy" are synonyms. Find the pairs of synonyms and draw a line connecting the two.

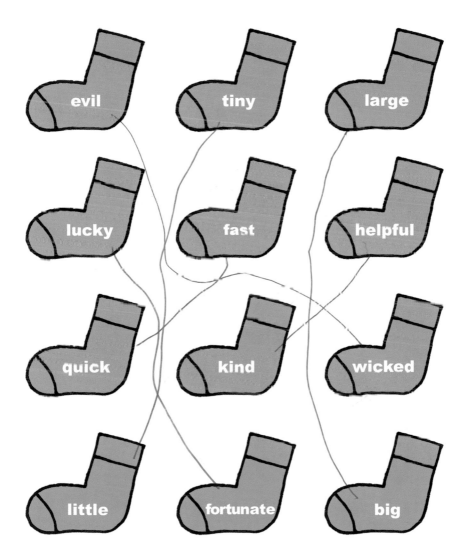

Acronyms 2

Acronyms are words formed from the initial letters of other words. For example **ASPS** could stand for "American Society Protecting Snakes."

Work out what the three acronyms could stand for, then make up one of your own at the end.

Theme: PUZZLES AND GAMES

Definitions 2

Choose the correct definition for each word.

Yak	1) An ox
	2) A sweet potato
	3) Something horrible
Mischief	1) The person in charge
	2) Naughtiness
	3) A problem
Pomegranate	1) Tropical fruit
	2) Small dog with silky fur
	3) Steel ball
Truffle	1) Something unimportant
	2) To sniff
	3) A fungus you can eat
Fierce	1) Woolly covering on an animal
	2) Violent or angry
	3) Scared

Leaping Lizard 2

The words of a sentence have been jumbled up and placed onto rocks. The lizard is sitting by the rock with the first word. Work out which order the words go in, and draw a line to show the lizard which way to jump.

You can write the sentence at the bottom.

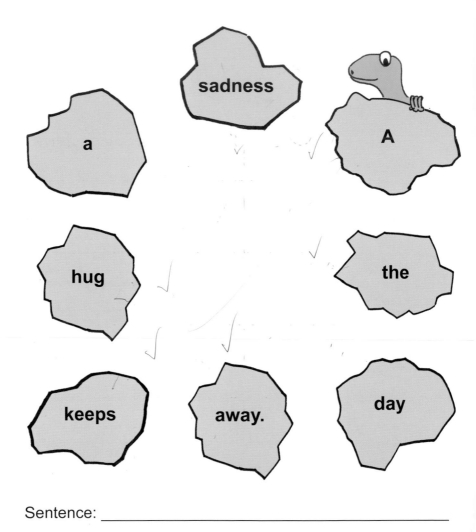

Sentence: _____

Syllables 2

Add a letter or letters to the ones already given to make words that are 1, 2, and 3 syllables long.
Note that the sound of the vowel may change, for example, "l<u>o</u>w" and "l<u>o</u>gic." That's okay.

	1 syllable	2 syllables	3 syllables
Mar	March	Margo	Marketyng
Le	leg	Leah	Levitate
Fa	Face	Fargo	Fathering
Con	Cone	Conway	Constitute

Compound Words 2

A compound word is formed when two words join together to become a new word; for example, softball, teapot, and armchair.

Draw lines between the two parts of the compound words.

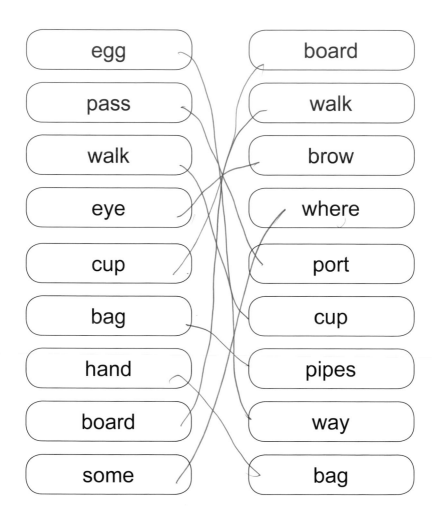

Continuous Words 2

This is a list of words joined together with the word spaces taken out. How many can you find?
Topic: INSECTS

**crickettermitecentipedebeebeetlespidersnaill
adybuggrubbutterflygrasshopperfleaantmag
gotmosquitomothcaterpillardragonflycockroa
chwasplocustcicada**

Speed Words 2

Choose words that fit the description. Use words that don't start with a capital letter, and use a different word for each question.

Choose a word that:

1	Rhymes with BEEF	reef
2	Fits into A __ __ __ E	Amore
3	Is an anagram of TERGA	
4	Has 7 letters	Jumping
5	Ends in "NER"	foreigner

60

Concentration 2

Either underline or put a circle around all the adjectives in the passage. Adjectives are words that describe nouns.

Wilma Wonders What to Do

Wilma was puzzled.

"What can I do to give that naughty boy a lesson?" she wondered.

"Cody!" she heard the boy's weary mother call. "If you don't stop being snotty I'll make you walk to the river and carry back a heavy bucket of water."

"You can't make me," rude Cody replied.

"Take the big blue bucket," his mom said, "and bring back plenty of fresh water."

"No!" Cody answered back, sitting down on the upturned blue bucket.

Vocabulary 2

Fit the three-letter words into the correct spaces in the larger words.

EAR   **ELF**   **END**   **ALE**   **OLD**   **OUT**

S _ _ _ E R

S _ _ _ S M A N

S _ _ _ C H

S _ _ _ H E R N

S _ _ _ I S H

S _ _ _ I E R

Change a Letter 2

Change one letter in the word so that it fits the definition.

Word	Definition	New word
TIRE	Thread of metal	WIRE
TIRE	Ripped	
TIRE	Movement of ocean	
SAW	Fasten with thread	SEW
SAW	Unhappy	SAD
SAW	A bone in the face	JAW
CORN	A baby is . . .	BORN
CORN	Round item of money	COIN
CORN	Center	CORE

Hat Words 2

Fill in the rows with words that begin with the letter A. Try not to use plurals.

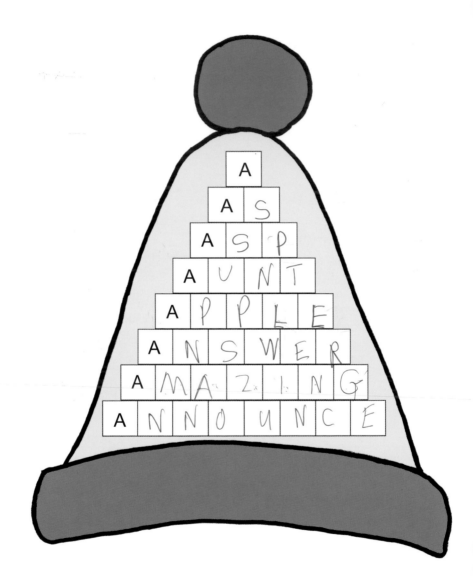

A

A S

A S P

A U N T

A P P L E

A N S W E R

A M A Z I N G

A N N O U N C E

Categories 2

The list contains words that fall into two categories: fruit and vegetables.
Write the words into the correct category in the balloons.

corn   lime   apple   pumpkin   pear   celery

banana   pea   carrot   tangerine   cabbage   peach

fruit

vegetables

Celery
pea
corrot
cabbag

Gridword 2

Place the words so they fit in the grid. Some letters have been filled in for you.

PORED
ELDER
PLUMP
DARED
PLEAD
UNDER

P	P	U	M	P
L	■	N	■	O
E	L	D	E	R
A	■	E	■	E
D	A	R	E	D

Lizard in a Cave 2

Each cave has an anagram of something to do with nature. Today the lizard wants to go in the cave with something that is **green**. Solve the anagrams and write the words beneath the caves, then color in or put a circle around the cave the lizard would like to go in.

CLOUD

WATER

GRASS

RIVER

BEACH

How Many 2

How many words can you think of that <u>only</u> contain one vowel, the letter **E**? The letter E can be anywhere in the word.
Aim for the number stated in each column, though you can do more if you like.

Words that contain the letter **E**		
1 E Aim for 10	2 E's Aim for 6	3 or more E's Aim for 2
River Blue Cruel well bell pencil belch hell hello kitchen	level bevel brulee cellmate feel peel	celebrate mastered deleted

Change and Rhyme 2

Change one letter in both words in the pair so they rhyme. For example, LIFT & WIRE becomes LIFE & WIFE.
There may be more than one solution.

SQUISH & POSE

SQUASH   POSH

BENT & HEAR

BEATT   HEAT

Q Crosswords 2

A straightforward crossword in the shape of a Q.

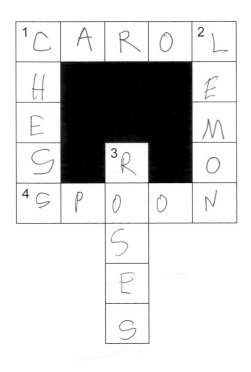

ACROSS
1. A song at Christmas
4. It's hard to eat soup without one of these

DOWN
1. A board game with king, queen, and bishop
2. Sour fruit
3. Red flower

Wheel Words 2

Work out what the word in each wheel reads. The letters go in a clockwise direction, and the word can start anywhere in the wheel.

Topic: FRUIT AND VEGETABLES

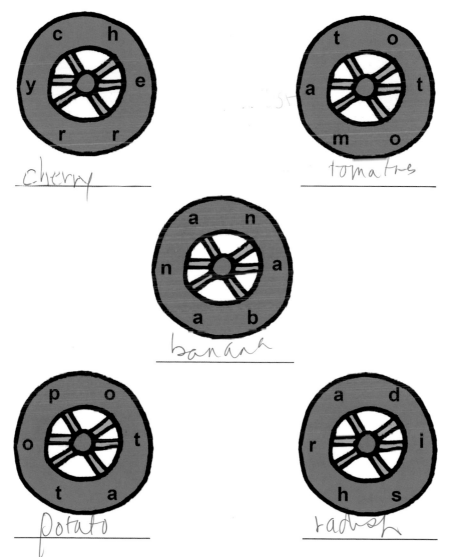

cherry

tomatoes

banana

potato

radish

Weird & Wonderful Words 2

Make a new compound word by choosing a word from each column and joining them together.
Write a description of what this new word means, and then write a sentence showing how it's used.

Top	nose
Silver	bell
Oven	breath
Book	friend
River	bee

WORD:

DESCRIPTION:

SENTENCE:

Remove a Letter 2

Take one letter out of each word so the words make a real sentence.
For example, if you take one letter out of each of these words, PIT HIS AN WHEN, it becomes IT IS A HEN.

THEN BONY SAWN HISS

JAUNT

AEIOU 2

The vowels A E I O U are missing from the following words.
Work out which vowel goes in which word, but check carefully
before you write them in!
Cross off the vowels as you use them.

P L U M   (A)

C O L D   (E)

S O A P   (I)

M E N   (O)

S U I T   (U)

Skillful Sentences 2

Can you write a sentence—or sentences—with at least four words, where all the words are four letters long?

In the Middle 2

Work out what word goes in the middle.

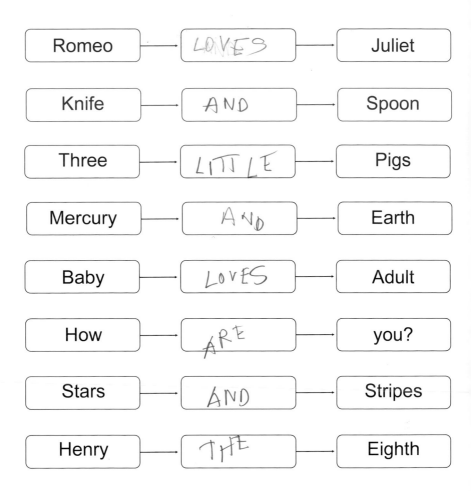

Romeo	LOVES	Juliet
Knife	AND	Spoon
Three	LITTLE	Pigs
Mercury	AND	Earth
Baby	LOVES	Adult
How	ARE	you?
Stars	AND	Stripes
Henry	THE	Eighth

Level 3

Word Line 3

Start at the letter in the circle and draw a continuous line right, left, up, or down (though not diagonally) to find the letters in the saying. The punctuation marks are not included.

"Why fit in when you were born to stand out?"
Dr. Seuss

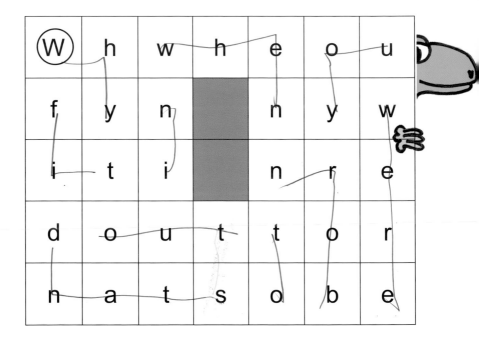

Umbrella Words 3

These umbrellas have letters on them. With the umbrella closed you can only see two letters. Work out words that might be written on the umbrella when it is open. The word has to contain these two letters in this order, but it can be as long or short as you like, and the letters can appear anywhere in the word. See if you can find different ways to include the letters in a word.

Train Words 3

Can you find the three-letter words hidden in the train cars?
Put a circle around them.

pat   tap   tin   nit   pot   top

Anagrams 3

Work out the anagrams, then draw a line between the words that are opposites.

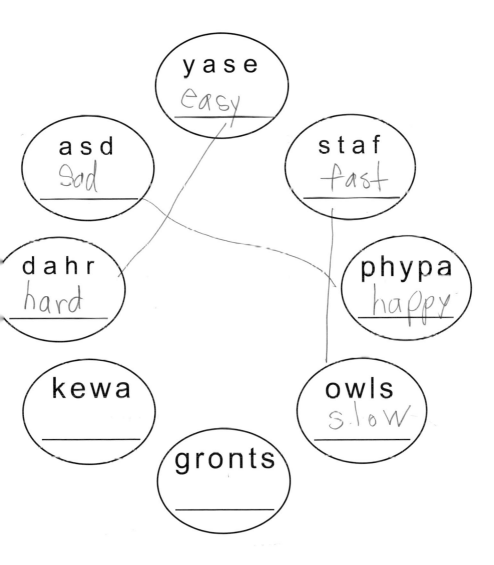

y a s e
easy

a s d
sad

s t a f
fast

d a h r
hard

phypa
happy

kewa
_____

owls
slow

gronts
_____

Alphabet Teasers 3

Choose words that fit into the grid using the letters given.

Begins with	Country	Flower, plant, or tree	Bird
C			
S			
F			
M			

Fishing 3

Fish for the right letters to make words that solve the clues.

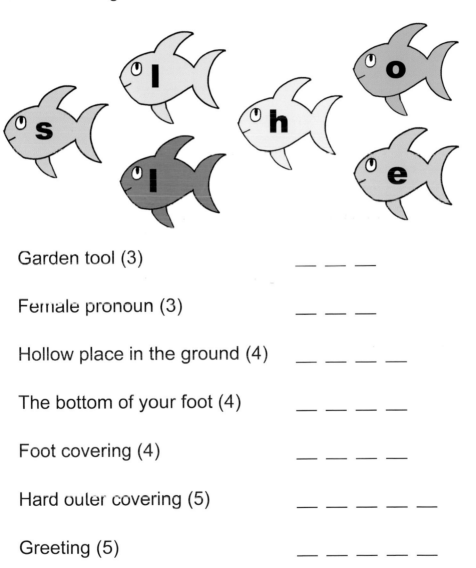

Garden tool (3)   — — —

Female pronoun (3)   — — —

Hollow place in the ground (4)   — — — —

The bottom of your foot (4)   — — — —

Foot covering (4)   — — — —

Hard outer covering (5)   — — — — —

Greeting (5)   — — — — —

Mini Word Sudoku 3

Write a letter from the four-letter word **"idea"** in each square so that each column, row, and mini-grid contains all the letters from the word.

		a	
a		e	
	a		e
	i		

Alphabet 3

Write these words in alphabetical order in the list.

elephant   mouse   _____

hound   elk   _____

vixen   warthog   _____

moose   jackal   _____

walrus   horse   _____

jaguar   viper   _____

_____

_____

_____

_____

_____

_____

Time to Rhyme 3

Write down five words, one in each petal, that rhyme with the word in the center.

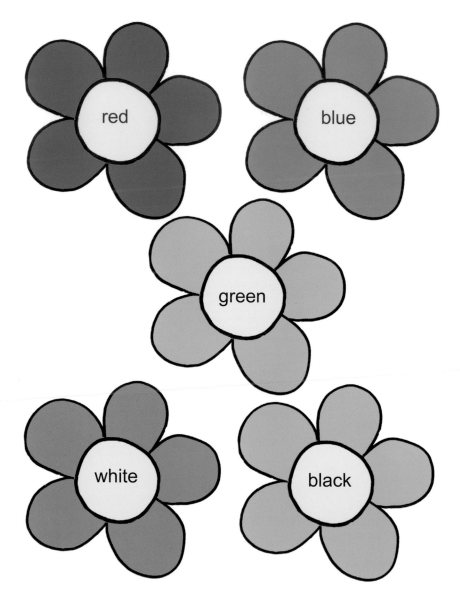

The Big X Word Search 3

The words to find are in pairs. You will find each pair of words in the shape of an X.

Can you find:
BORED - TIRED
DAZED - DIZZY
TOUGH - ROUGH
BRAVE - SHARP
HAPPY - SUPER

B	N	I	T	S	T	F	A	G	M	T
C	R	T	H	T	A	I	T	P	J	M
K	R	A	B	A	P	T	T	K	J	R
A	R	C	V	O	J	I	O	V	O	A
P	K	C	C	E	R	K	I	U	A	C
E	M	A	M	E	R	E	G	D	G	A
H	M	F	D	S	M	H	D	R	M	H
H	A	M	U	A	T	I	A	P	A	S
A	D	P	A	W	Z	K	M	S	S	C
F	E	W	P	Z	K	E	C	S	F	M
R	C	D	Y	Y	A	T	D	I	C	C

The Word Store 3

The Word Store is a special place that sells different kinds of words. Today we are going shopping for **adjectives** (describing words). Wherever there is a space in the story, write in an adjective that starts with the letter given. It's a good idea to read through the story first to get a feel for what you may want to write. If you write in pencil, you can do the puzzle more than once and make the story different each time.

The Word Store

Liz's teacher was a _____ !

Never before had her teacher seen such a piece of i _____ writing.

"This is g _____ work," he told Liz. "You should think about becoming a novelist. You are extremely t _____. Your parents will be d _____ when they read this w _____ essay."

Liz felt e _____. She hadn't realized she had ability; she just felt o_____.

But the comment from her teacher had made her feel more c_____.

"Who knows?" she thought. "Maybe one day I'll be f_____!"

Letters 3

Color the squares with **consonants** in **blue**.
Color the squares with **vowels** in **pink**.
Then work out what the picture is.

o	u	a	e	o	a	i	e	i	o
d	j	i	a	s	g	o	c	j	u
l	p	u	o	b	w	e	l	p	a
c	y	a	e	l	y	o	a	i	u
s	b	r	s	j	s	i	l	w	e
d	j	g	c	p	d	e	g	h	o
p	l	a	u	w	r	a	y	c	u
w	c	u	o	g	r	u	l	j	i
g	l	i	e	y	j	e	s	r	a
v	i	a	o	i	e	a	i	e	o

Words and Sounds 3

Homophones are words that are spelled and pronounced the same, but have different meanings.

The story below contains two words that are pronounced the same, though only one of them has the right meaning in the sentence. Cross off the wrong one.

Bike riding

"Don't
| brake |
| break |
your neck!" yelled Mom as Johnny
| rode |
| road |

down the
| rode |
| road |
quickly. "Avoid the
| whole |
| hole |
in the ground."

"The
| mane |
| main |
street is okay!" Johnny called back. "And

anyway, I'm a
| grate |
| great |
cyclist!"

Mom raised her eyebrows. "He'll
| wail |
| whale |
and
| wine |
| whine |
if he

falls off." Last time he did that he was in
| pane |
| pain |
for
| days. |
| daze. |

"Keep your feet on the
| pedals!" |
| peddles!" |
she called after him.

Synonyms 3

A synonym is a word that means exactly or nearly the same as another word; for example, "sad" and "unhappy" are synonyms. Find the pairs of synonyms and draw a line connecting the two.

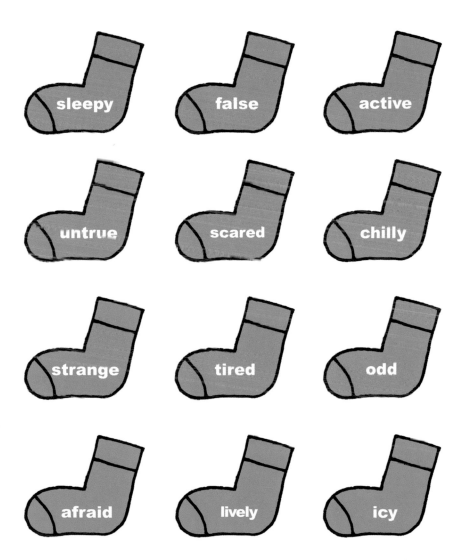

sleepy   false   active

untrue   scared   chilly

strange   tired   odd

afraid   lively   icy

Acronyms 3

Acronyms are words formed from the initial letters of other words. For example **ASPS** could stand for "American Society Protecting Snakes."

Work out what the three acronyms could stand for, then make up one of your own at the end.

Theme: BOOKS

Definitions 3

Choose the correct definition for each word.

Baboon	1) A fruit 2) A large monkey 3) Meaningless sounds
Globe	1) The planet earth 2) Part of the ear 3) Shiny and bright
Millennium	1) Worthless person 2) Person who makes hats 3) One thousand years
Colossal	1) Huge 2) Statue 3) Person living in a colony
Intricate	1) To point 2) Complicated 3) To point out

Leaping Lizard 3

The words of a sentence have been jumbled up and placed onto rocks. The lizard is sitting by the rock with the first word. Work out which order the words go in, and draw a line to show the lizard which way to jump.
You can write the sentence at the bottom.

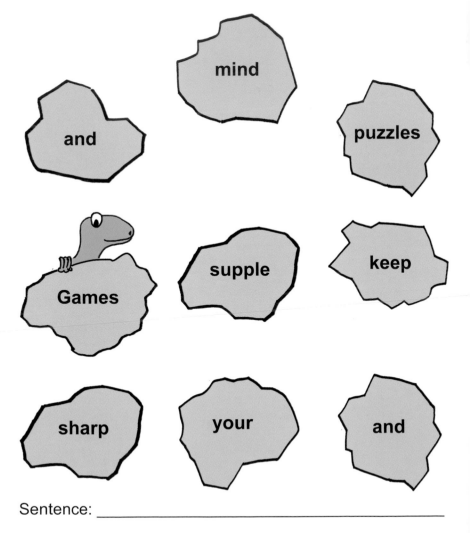

Sentence: _____

Syllables 3

Add a letter or letters to the ones already given to make words that are 1, 2, and 3 syllables long.

Note that the sound of the vowel may change; for example, "l<u>o</u>w" and "l<u>o</u>gic." That's okay.

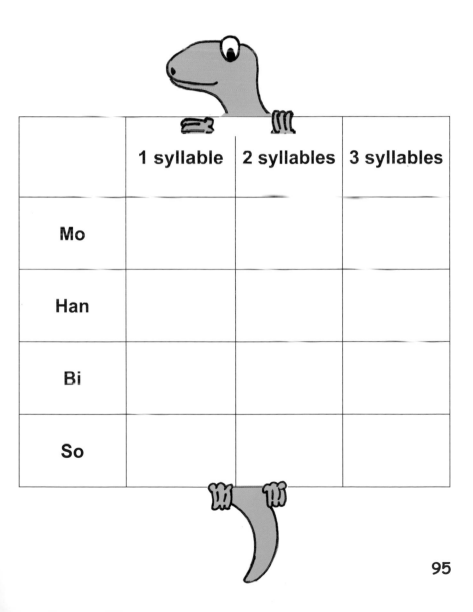

	1 syllable	2 syllables	3 syllables
Mo			
Han			
Bi			
So			

Compound Words 3

A compound word is formed when two words join together to become a new word; for example, softball, teapot, and armchair.

Draw lines between the two parts of the compound words.

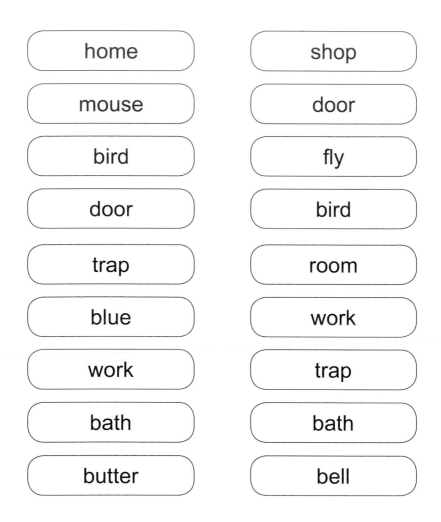

home	shop
mouse	door
bird	fly
door	bird
trap	room
blue	work
work	trap
bath	bath
butter	bell

Continuous Words 3

This is a list of words joined together with the word spaces taken out. How many can you find?
Topic: COLORS

**goldredgreenmaroonbrownindigoorangeg
rayyellowwhitecreammauvepurplescarletviol
etturquoisebluesilverlilacblacklavenderburg
undypinklimeteal**

Speed Words 3

Choose words that fit the description. Use words that don't start with a capital letter and use a different word for each question.

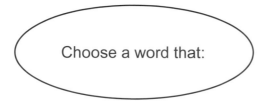

Choose a word that:

1	Has 5 letters and ends in N	
2	Is an anagram of ALERT and ALTER	
3	Contains 3 vowels	
4	Has 6 letters including MM	
5	Has 4 letters and starts with Z	

Concentration 3

Either underline or put a circle around the definite article (the word "the") in the passage.

Wilma Gets It Right

Wilma smiled and got out her magic wand. Instantly, the boy's shoes came to life and Cody jumped up. He picked up the blue bucket and ran wildly to the river. He staggered back with a heavy bucket of water.

"Stop!" shouted Cody. "Someone stop these shoes!"

"You are being silly," scolded his mom. "Shoes do not run on their own."

Back and forth the shoes ran to the river with Cody inside them, struggling to carry the blue bucket, which seemed to get heavier each time.

"I'm sorry, I'm sorry!" he shouted to his mom. "I've learned my lesson. I'll be good for the rest of the day!"

Mom raised her eyebrows. "Okay," she said, feeling bewildered.

Wilma smiled, and the shoes stopped moving.

Vocabulary 3

Fit the three-letter words into the correct spaces in the larger words.

PAD   PAN   PAT   PEA   POW   PUP

__ __ __ E R

__ __ __ T E R N

__ __ __ P E T

__ __ __ D L E

__ __ __ C H

__ __ __ I C

Change a Letter 3

Change one letter in the word so it fits the definition.

Word	Definition	New word
SALE	Secure	
SALE	White substance	
SALE	Man	
TAIL	Letters and packages	
TAIL	High	
TAIL	Icy rain	
LAZE	Slow moving	
LAZE	Large pond	
LAZE	Confusing place	

Hat Words 3

Fill in the rows with words that begin with the letters A through H. Try not to use plurals.

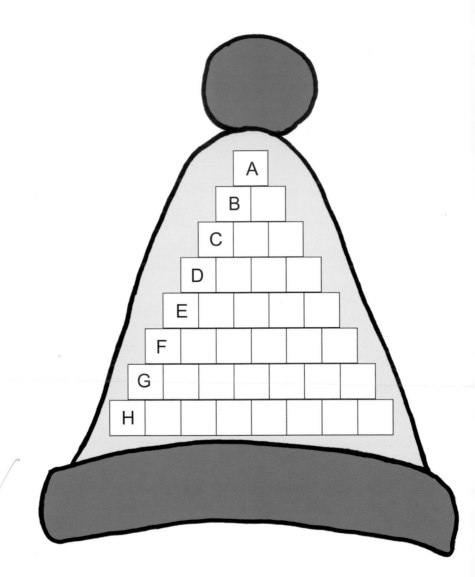

Categories 3

The list contains words that fall into three categories: mammal, sea creature, and bird.
Write the words into the correct category in the balloons.

giraffe   thrush   hare   stingray   swallow   eagle

squid   wolf   eel   owl   lobster   koala

mammal   sea creature   bird

Gridword 3

Place the words so they fit in the grid. Two letters have been filled in for you.

NOVEL
MINER
ROLES
MINIM
MARES
NEVER

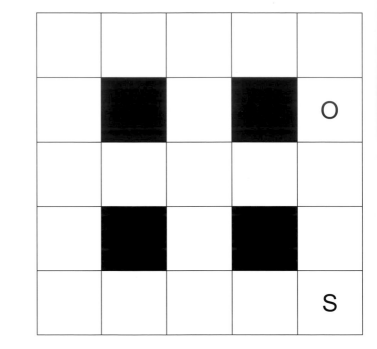

Lizard in a Cave 3

Each cave has an anagram of an item that has a particular shape.

Today the lizard wants to go in the cave with something that is **round**. Solve the anagrams and write the words beneath the caves, then color in or put a circle around the cave the lizard would like to go in.

How Many 3

How many words can you think of that <u>only</u> contain one vowel, the letter I? The letter I can be anywhere in the word.
Aim for the number stated in each column, though you can do more if you like.

Words that contain the letter I		
1 I Aim for 10	2 I's Aim for 2	3 or more I's Aim for 1

Change and Rhyme 3

Change one letter in both words in the pair so they rhyme. For example, LIFT & WIRE becomes LIFE & WIFE.
There may be more than one solution.

SCENE & WEST

NETS & LOST

Q Crosswords 3

A straightforward crossword in the shape of a Q.

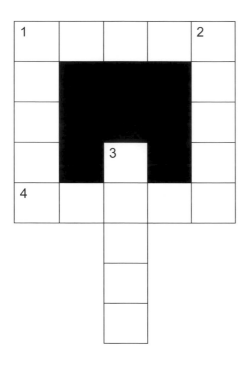

ACROSS
1. Ridiculous, funny
4. Part of a flower

DOWN
1. Nighttime rest
2. An unusual way to sing
3. An envelope may need one of these

Wheel Words 3

Work out what the word in each wheel reads. The letters go in a clockwise direction, and the word can start anywhere in the wheel.

Topic: COLORS

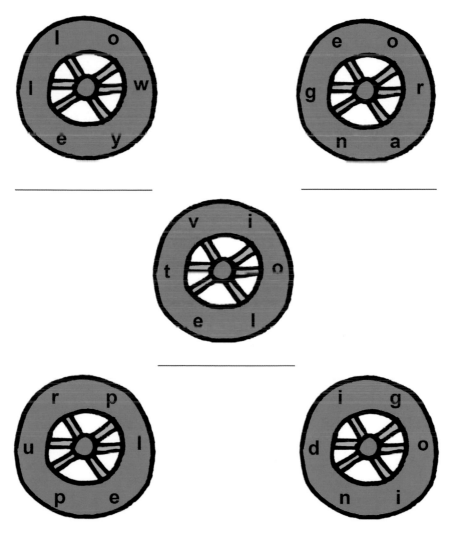

Weird & Wonderful Words 3

Make a new compound word by choosing a word from each column and joining them together.
Write a description of what this new word means, and then write a sentence showing how it's used.

Dream	bag
Door	stick
Eye	pen
Spin	circle
Smile	boot

WORD:

DESCRIPTION:

SENTENCE:

Remove a Letter 3

Take one letter out of each word so the words make a proper sentence.
For example, if you take one letter out of each of these words, PIT HIS AN WHEN, it becomes IT IS A HEN.

IT HAVEN AT KNEW PELT

AEIOU 3

The vowels A E I O U are missing from the following words. Work out which vowel goes in which word, but check carefully before you write them in!
Cross off the vowels as you use them.

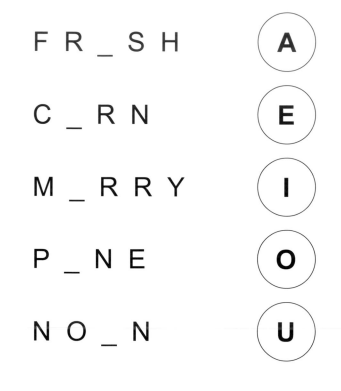

F R _ S H   A

C _ R N   E

M _ R R Y   I

P _ N E   O

N O _ N   U

Skillful Sentences 3

Can you write a sentence—or sentences—with at least four words, where all the words start with a different letter of the alphabet? Start with the letter A, go onto B, and see how far you get.

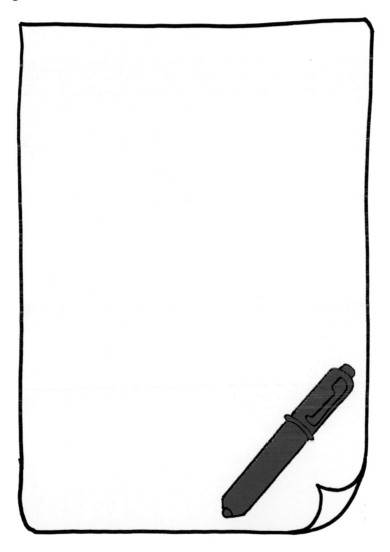

In the Middle 3

Work out what word goes in the middle.

Three		Men
Just		Time
Jack		Jill
Bad		Worst
Peace		Earth
Rio		Janeiro
President		Obama
Whole		Quarter

Level 4

Word Line 4

Start at the letter in the circle and draw a continuous line right, left, up, or down (though not diagonally) to find the letters in the saying. The punctuation marks are not included.

"The time is always right to do what is right."
Martin Luther King, Jr.

t	t	i	m	e	r	i
h	e	a	s	i	s	g
g	h	l	w	a	y	h
i	(T)	t	a	o	d	t
r	s	i	h	w	o	t

Umbrella Words 4

These umbrellas have letters on them. With the umbrella closed you can only see two letters. Work out words that might be written on the umbrella when it is open. The word has to contain these two letters in this order, but it can be as long or short as you like, and the letters can appear anywhere in the word. See if you can find different ways to include the letters in a word.

c h

e l

p a

s t

Train Words 4

Can you find the three-letter words hidden in the train cars?
Put a circle around them.

ode   odd   ore   owe   owl   one

Anagrams 4

Work out the anagrams, then draw a line between the words that are opposites.

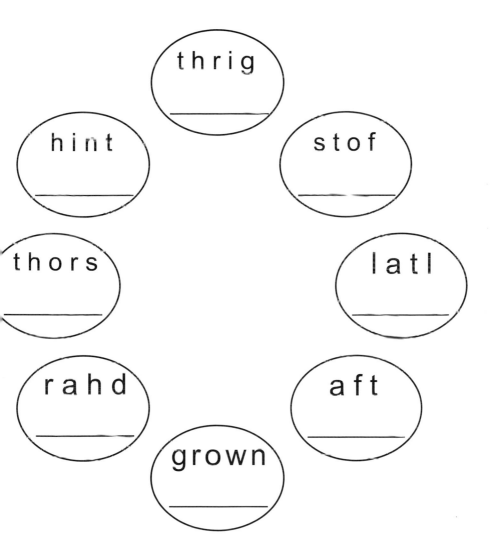

Alphabet Teasers 4

Choose words that fit into the grid using the letters given.

Begins with	Item in kitchen	Item in bathroom	Item in bedroom
S			
B			
T			
M			

Fishing 4

Fish for the right letters to make words that solve the clues.

Color (3)   — — —

Insect (3)   — — —

Small animal/rodent (3)   — — —

Close by (4)   — — — —

Small arrow (4)   — — — —

Expensive (4)   — — — —

Walk (5)   — — — — —

Mini Word Sudoku 4

Write a letter from the four-letter word **"grid"** in each square so that each column, row, and mini-grid contains all the letters from the word.

	g	i	
r			
			i
	r	g	

Alphabet 4

Put these words in <u>reverse</u> alphabetical order in the list below. Use the alphabet to help you: **a b c d e f g h i j k l m n o p q r s t u v w x y z**

handsome	nosey	_____
sickly	tired	_____
brash	quaint	_____
noisy	brave	_____
timid	happy	_____
silly	quiet	_____
		_____
		_____
		_____
		_____
		_____

Time to Rhyme 4

Write down five words, one in each petal, that rhyme with the word in the center.

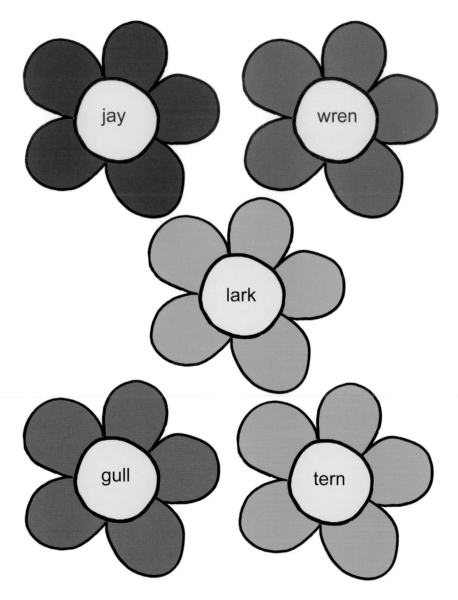

The Big X Word Search 4

The words to find are in pairs. You will find each pair of words in the shape of an X.

Can you find:
DAVID - ALVIN
AARON - BARRY
BOBBY - ROBIN
BRIAN - CLIVE
HENRY - KENNY

K	A	S	G	H	R	L	D	V	B	E
D	E	N	E	O	D	O	B	O	W	S
S	T	N	W	M	P	Q	D	C	S	H
K	R	U	N	E	O	B	P	I	A	S
Y	D	F	B	Y	Y	D	A	G	N	A
H	J	K	L	A	Z	A	A	X	L	C
V	B	B	N	M	R	C	Q	V	W	E
R	T	Y	R	O	L	R	I	U	I	I
O	P	A	N	I	S	N	Y	D	F	D
G	H	J	V	K	A	L	Z	X	C	V
B	N	E	M	A	S	N	D	F	G	H

The Word Store 4

The Word Store is a special place that sells different kinds of words. Today we are going shopping for **nouns** (person, place, or thing). Wherever there is a space in the story, write in a noun that starts with the letter given. It's a good idea to read through the story first to get a feel for what you may want to write. If you write in pencil, you can do the puzzle more than once and make the story different each time.

The Word Store

"I can't find my c _____!" shouted Jack. "Can I borrow somebody's p _____ instead?"

Lily looked at him. "Jack, you could lose anything, even your h _____ if you aren't careful!"

Jack smiled. "Last week I lost my w _____ and my j _____."

"You're a d _____," laughed Lily. "If I gave you a m _____ you would probably drop it on the f _____!"

"My brother wanted to give me a c _____ for my birthday," said Jack, "but changed his mind and gave me a b _____ instead."

Letters 4

Color the squares with **consonants** in **brown**.
Color the squares with **vowels** in **blue**.
Then work out what the picture is.

Q	B	W	Y	F	R	Q	D	V	Y
D	O	I	U	R	G	O	U	I	H
F	E	A	E	H	B	A	E	U	C
V	I	O	A	G	Y	E	I	A	R
W	B	Q	D	C	H	D	Q	W	F
C	Y	G	W	V	R	Y	H	C	B
H	E	O	U	G	F	O	E	O	D
F	I	U	A	V	B	A	I	A	H
Q	A	E	O	R	C	E	U	I	V
W	C	Q	D	F	B	V	H	Y	W

Words and Sounds 4

In each sentence there is a word with a silent letter. Write this letter in the box at the end. The letters in the boxes will spell another word.

Silent letter

The man lost his comb.

The guest left the room.

Jan is in the final scene.

He hit my knee with a bat.

Do not talk to me yet.

I got pie and chips.

Synonyms 4

A synonym is a word that means exactly or nearly the same as another word; for example, "sad" and "unhappy" are synonyms. Find the pairs of synonyms and draw a line connecting the two.

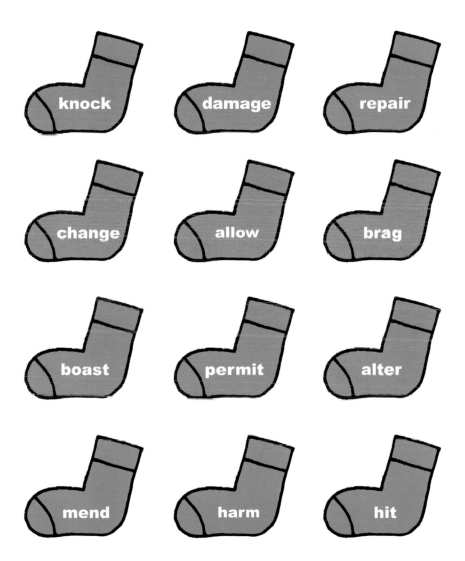

Acronyms 4

Acronyms are words formed from the initial letters of other words. For example **ASPS** could stand for "American Society Protecting Snakes."

Work out what the three acronyms could stand for, then make up one of your own at the end.

Theme: SPORTS

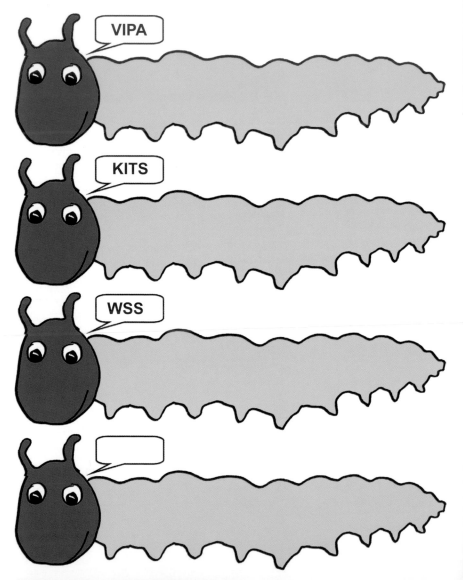

Definitions 4

Choose the correct definition for each word.

Siesta	1) Mountain range 2) Reddish-brown color 3) Afternoon nap
Wallaby	1) Small kangaroo 2) To hit or beat 3) Type of buffalo
Oboe	1) Very large 2) Woodwind instrument 3) To do what you are told
Miracle	1) Something that seems to be real, but isn't there 2) Extremely unusual and wonderful event 3) Very small
Radish	1) A vegetable 2) Gentle breeze 3) Large airship

Leaping Lizard 4

The words of a sentence have been jumbled up and placed onto rocks. The lizard is sitting by the rock with the first word. Work out which order the words go in, and draw a line to show the lizard which way to jump.

You can write the sentence at the bottom.

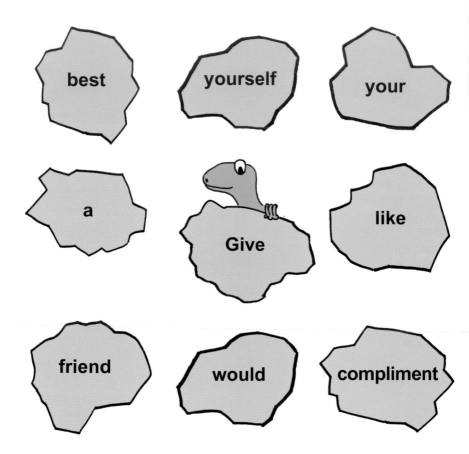

best

yourself

your

a

Give

like

friend

would

compliment

Sentence: _____

Syllables 4

Add a letter or letters to the ones already given to make words that are 1, 2, and 3 syllables long.
Note that the sound of the vowel may change; for example, "l<u>o</u>w" and "l<u>o</u>gic." That's okay.

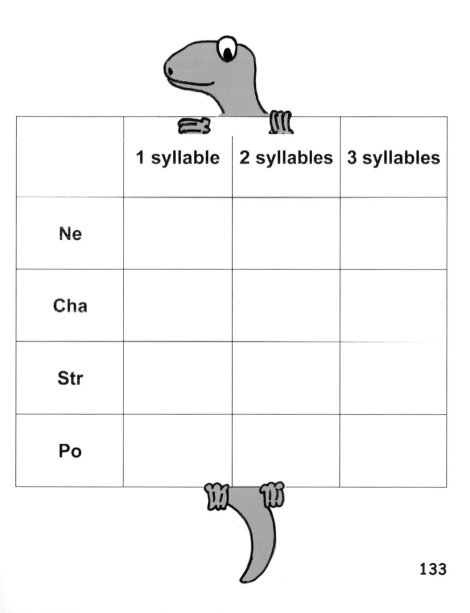

	1 syllable	2 syllables	3 syllables
Ne			
Cha			
Str			
Po			

Compound Words 4

A compound word is formed when two words join together to become a new word; for example, softball, teapot, and armchair.

Think of as many words as you can that could join onto the <u>end</u> of the given word to make a compound word. An example has been given for you.

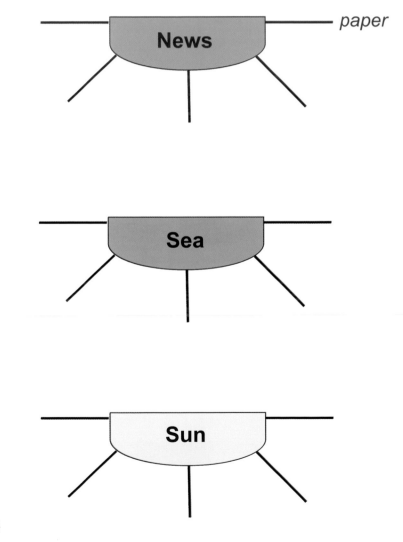

Continuous Words 4

This is a list of words joined together with the word spaces taken out. How many can you find?
Topic: ITEMS OF CLOTHING

**bootsskirttrousersscarfshoesdressshirtsuitt
ievestbeltblazerglovesshortsslacksblouses
lipperssockspajamassweatersneakersunde
rpantssandalsjeansjackethatcoatcardiganca
poveralls**

Speed Words 4

Choose words that fit the description. Use words that don't start with a capital letter, and use a different word for each question.

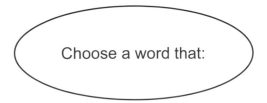

Choose a word that:

1	Rhymes with THEFT	
2	Contains 2 U's anywhere in the word	
3	Has 6 letters and starts with W	
4	Fits into M __ __ __ __ R	
5	Has 3 syllables and is a type of animal	

Concentration 4

Either underline or put a circle around all the pronouns in the passage. A pronoun is a word in place of a noun; for example, "we."

Wilma and the Wizard

The following week Wilma went to see Wilfred the Wizard.

"Will you show me how to make a new potion?" she asked him.

"Certainly," he replied. "Tell me what you want."

"A potion to turn you and me into a prince and a princess," she said.

They looked through the potion book together. He chose the best potion, and they turned into a handsome prince and a beautiful princess.

"Will you marry me?" he asked.

"No," she replied. "Instead, we will go off on an adventure!"

Vocabulary 4

Fit the three-letter words into the correct spaces in the larger words.

ANY   AWE   ALL   ARM   ARE   ARC

_ _ _ O W S

_ _ _ O N E

_ _ _ H E R Y

_ _ _ P I T

_ _ _ N A

_ _ _ S O M E

Change a Letter 4

Change one letter in the word so it fits the definition.

Word	Definition	New word
BASS	To give orders to	
BASS	Church service	
BASS	Flying creatures	
HARP	Difficult	
HARP	Small rabbit-like mammal	
HARP	Damage	
FORE	Shoot a bullet	
FORE	Middle of an apple	
FORE	Eating implement	

Hat Words 4

Fill in the rows with words that begin with the letter S. Try not to use plurals.

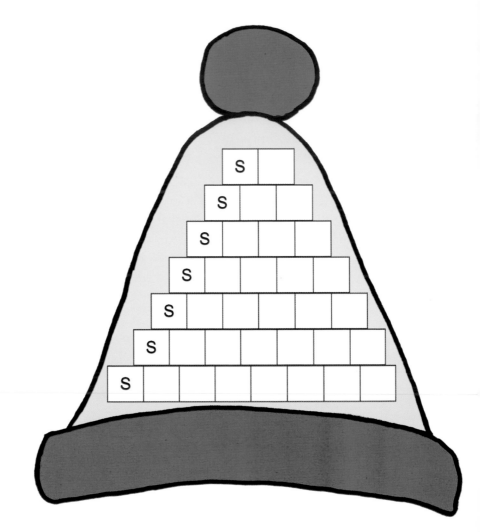

Categories 4

The list contains words that fall into three categories: adjective, adverb, and noun.
Write the words into the correct category in the balloons.

honest   happily   eager   honesty   eagerness
eagerly   honestly   happy   happiness

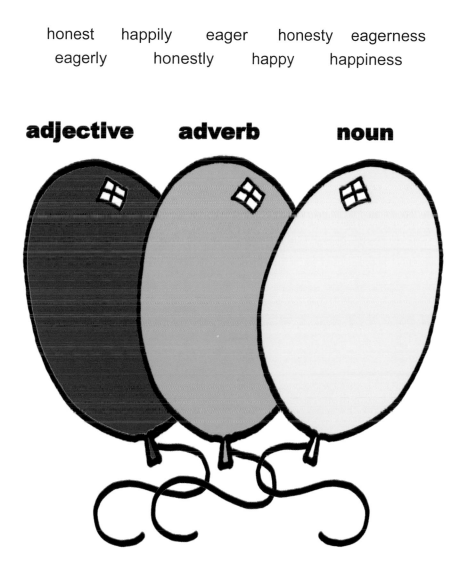

adjective   **adverb**   **noun**

Gridword 4

Place the words so they fit in the grid. A letter has been filled in for you.

TROUT
EIDER
TAROT
SLEET
RODEO
STRUT

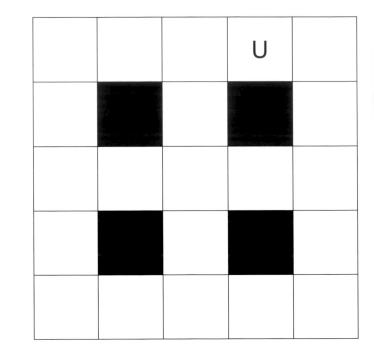

Lizard in a Cave 4

Each cave has an anagram of a person's name.
Today the lizard wants to go in the cave with a boy. Solve the
anagrams and write the words beneath the caves, then color
in or put a circle around the cave the lizard would like to go in.

How Many 4

How many words can you think of that <u>only</u> contain one vowel, the letter **O**? The letter O can be anywhere in the word.
Aim for the number stated in each column, though you can do more if you like.

Words that contain the letter **O**		
1 O Aim for 10	2 O's Aim for 6	3 or more O's Aim for 1

Change and Rhyme 4

Change one letter in both words in the pair so they rhyme. For example, LIFT & WIRE becomes LIFE & WIFE.
There may be more than one solution.

WHOSE & BAWL

RUDE & FOWL

Q Crosswords 4

A straightforward crossword in the shape of a Q.

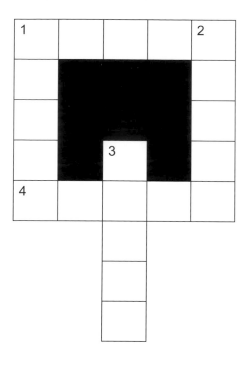

ACROSS
1. Worn around the neck
4. Hopefully your teacher will do this

DOWN
1. Begin
2. Not stale
3. Meat similar to ham

Wheel Words 4

Work out what the word in each wheel reads. The letters go in a clockwise direction, and the word can start anywhere in the wheel.

Topic: BIRDS

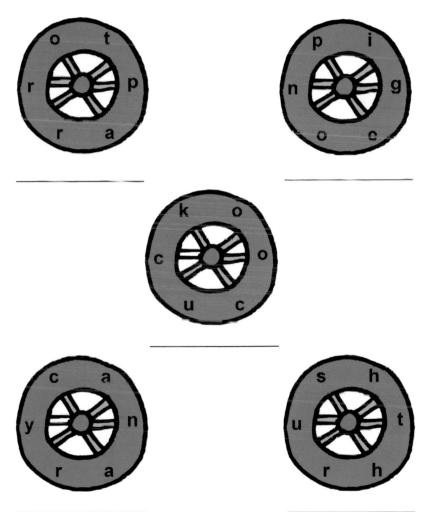

_____

_____

_____

Weird & Wonderful Words 4

Make a new compound word by choosing a word from each column and joining them together.
Write a description of what this new word means, and then write a sentence showing how it's used.

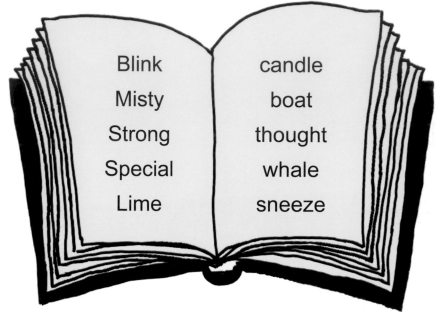

Blink	candle
Misty	boat
Strong	thought
Special	whale
Lime	sneeze

WORD:

DESCRIPTION:

SENTENCE:

Remove a Letter 4

Take one letter out of each word so the words make a real sentence.
For example, if you take one letter out of each of these words, PIT HIS AN WHEN, it becomes IT IS A HEN.

LEFT'S GOT TOE THEN

SPARK

A E I O U 4

The vowels A E I O U are missing from the following words. Work out which vowel goes in which word, but check carefully before you write them in!
Cross off the vowels as you use them.

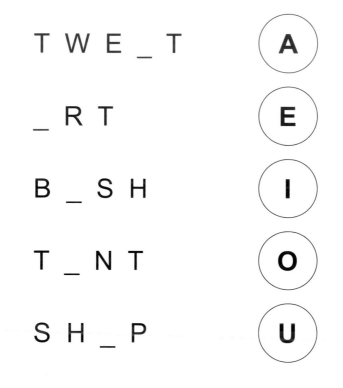

T W E _ T   (A)

_ R T   (E)

B _ S H   (I)

T _ N T   (O)

S H _ P   (U)

Skillful Sentences 4

Can you write a sentence—or sentences—with at least four words, where the last letter of one word is the same as the first letter of the next word?

In the Middle 4

Work out what word goes in the middle.

Three		Mice
Over		Out
Yellow		Road
New		City
Morning		Evening
Caterpillar		Butterfly
Bacon		Tomato
Bird		Prey

Level 5

Word Line 5

Start at the letter in the circle and draw a continuous line right, left, up, or down (though not diagonally) to find the letters in the saying. The punctuation marks are not included.

"No one is perfect . . . that's why pencils have erasers."
Wolfgang Reibe

r	e	s	a	e	v	s	l
s	f	e	r	e	a	h	i
(N)	r	c	t	t	e	n	c
o	e	p	s	h	p	y	h
o	n	e	i	a	t	s	w

Umbrella Words 5

These umbrellas have letters on them. With the umbrella closed you can only see two letters. Work out words that might be written on the umbrella when it is open. The word has to contain these two letters in this order, but it can be as long or short as you like, and the letters can appear anywhere in the word. See if you can find different ways to include the letters in a word.

Train Words 5

Can you find the 3-letter words hidden in the train cars? Put a circle around them.

rim   rip   rib   rid   bid   rig

Anagrams 5

Work out the anagrams, then draw a line between the words that are opposites.

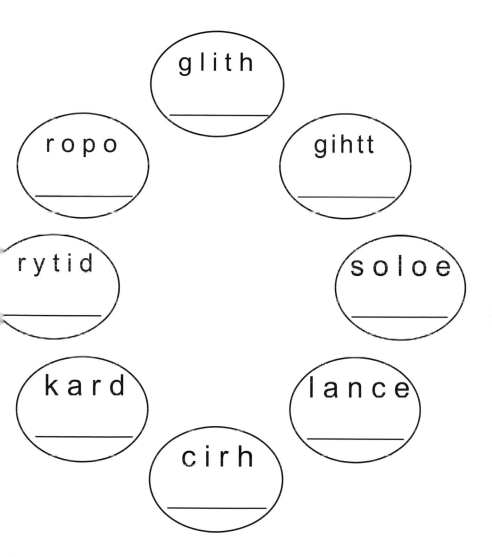

Alphabet Teasers 5

Choose words that fit into the grid using the letters given.

Begins with	Relative	Insect	Fruit
G			
S			
A			
M			

Fishing 5

Fish for the right letters to make words that solve the clues.

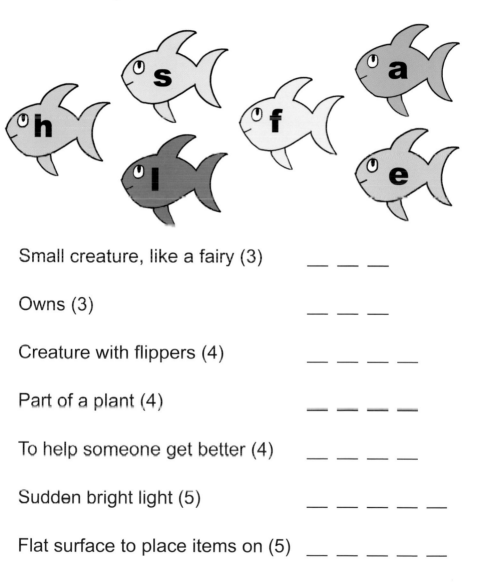

Small creature, like a fairy (3)   __ __ __

Owns (3)   __ __ __

Creature with flippers (4)   __ __ __ __

Part of a plant (4)   __ __ __ __

To help someone get better (4)   __ __ __ __

Sudden bright light (5)   __ __ __ __ __

Flat surface to place items on (5)   __ __ __ __ __

Mini Word Sudoku 5

Write a letter from the four-letter word **"maze"** in each square so that each column, row, and mini-grid contains all the letters from the word.

a			
		z	
	e		
			m

Alphabet 5

Put a circle around the words with letters in alphabetical order. Use the alphabet to help you: **a b c d e f g h i j k l m n o p q r s t u v w x y z**

rut	beg	try	hip
gin	bed	lie	opt
sup	art	fry	hid
gel	pot	boy	row
lot	bow	dab	den

Time to Rhyme 5

Write down five words, one in each petal, that rhyme with the word in the center.

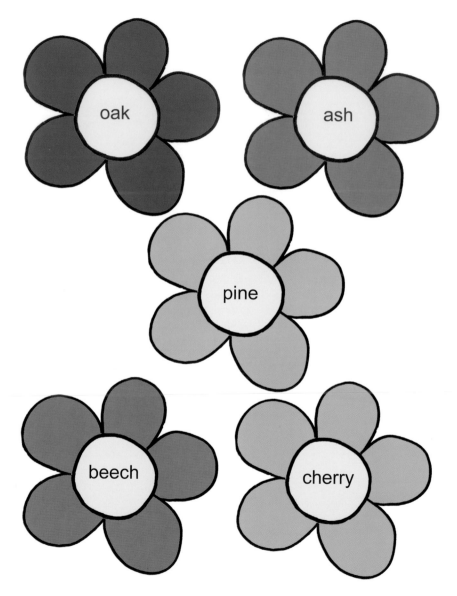

The Big X Word Search 5

The words to find are in pairs. You will find each pair of words in the shape of an X.

Can you find:
LARRY - MARIO
MATEO - ANTON
JACOB - OSCAR
LOGAN - ROGER
LLOYD - SCOTT

P	O	I	U	Y	T	R	R	E	W	L
M	Q	L	K	A	J	H	O	G	O	F
D	A	S	N	A	M	N	B	G	V	C
X	Z	T	P	O	I	U	A	Y	E	T
M	O	R	E	I	F	N	W	Q	L	R
N	A	K	A	O	J	O	H	G	F	J
D	S	R	A	L	M	N	S	S	A	B
V	R	C	I	X	L	Z	C	C	P	O
Y	I	U	Y	O	T	O	O	R	A	E
W	Q	L	J	H	T	B	Y	G	F	R
D	S	A	L	T	K	J	H	D	G	F

The Word Store 5

The Word Store is a special place that sells different kinds of words. Today we are going shopping for **nouns** (person, place, or thing). Wherever there is a space in the story, write in a noun that starts with the letter given. It's a good idea to read through the story first to get a feel for what you may want to write. If you write in pencil, you can do the puzzle more than once and make the story different each time.

"There are only b _____ and sandwiches in the picnic basket," said Joy. "Has anyone got any c_____ as well?"

"I've got some a _____ and some g _____," said Phil.

"Did someone bring j _____?" asked Joy.

"Let me go to the k _____ and see if we have any," said Jackie.

She looked in the c _____ and even behind the m _____ but couldn't find any.

"I've found some w _____. Will that do?" she asked.

"Yes, great. Let's go," replied Joy.

Letters 5

Color the squares with **capital letters** in **gray**.
Color the squares with **lower case letters** in **green**.
Then work out what the picture is.

g	t	r	h	t	u	d	z	w	u
k	f	c	y	w	r	c	M	K	k
p	t	f	o	z	p	o	H	S	g
f	o	w	y	d	e	w	W	Y	u
c	h	e	d	u	k	t	L	P	z
y	z	Z	U	M	W	F	K	S	f
k	y	Y	P	S	H	F	Q	N	h
e	g	Q	K	c	z	e	W	Z	p
w	u	M	H	k	h	o	U	L	u
c	t	Y	L	p	t	h	Y	F	y

Words and Sounds 5

In each sentence there is a word with a silent letter. Write this
letter in the box at the end. The letters in the boxes will spell
another word.

Silent letter

She ran past the castle.

T

He left six hours ago.

H

That's my old guitar.

U

It's windy in autumn.

N

Dad wants a sandwich.

D

Do not come in yet.

E

It's a hot iron.

R

Synonyms 5

A synonym is a word that means exactly or nearly the same as another word; for example, "sad" and "unhappy" are synonyms. Find the pairs of synonyms and draw a line connecting the two.

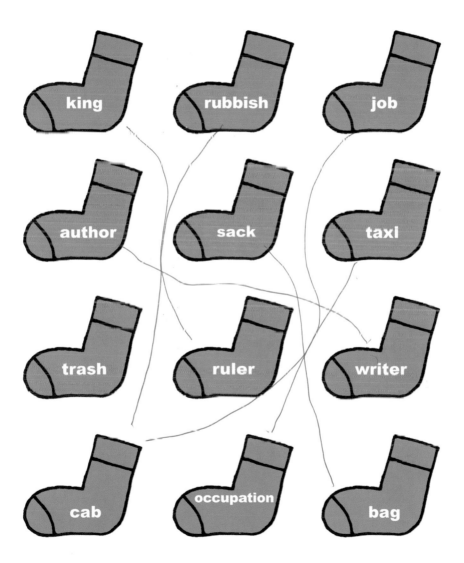

king   rubbish   job

author   sack   taxi

trash   ruler   writer

cab   occupation   bag

Acronyms 5

Acronyms are words formed from the initial letters of other words. For example, **ASPS** could stand for "American Society Protecting Snakes."

Work out what the three acronyms could stand for, then make up one of your own at the end.

Theme: CREATIVE GROUPS

Definitions 5

Choose the correct definition for each word.

Jackal	1)	Wild animal
	2)	Book cover
	3)	Man who does repair work
Braille	1)	Plaited hair
	2)	System of writing for people who are blind
	3)	A flat fish
Identical	1)	The very same
	2)	Picture of person described by witness
	3)	Having strong teeth
Audible	1)	Believable
	2)	Awful
	3)	Something you can hear
Smog	1)	Heavy fog
	2)	Child's clothing
	3)	Small cat

Leaping Lizard 5

The words of a sentence have been jumbled up and placed onto rocks. The lizard is sitting by the rock with the first word. Work out which order the words go in, and draw a line to show the lizard which way to jump.
You can write the sentence at the bottom.

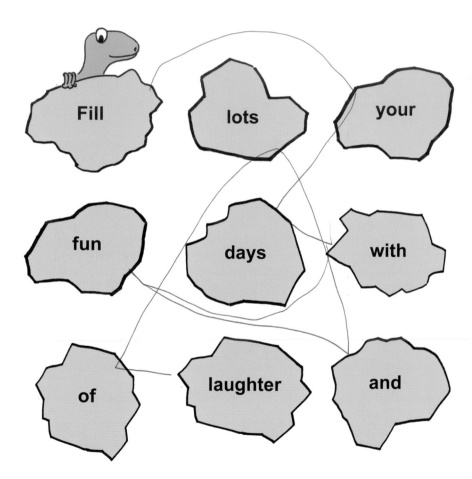

Sentence: _____

Syllables 5

Add a letter or letters to the ones already given to make words that are 1, 2, and 3 syllables long.
Note that the sound of the vowel may change; for example, "l<u>o</u>w" and "l<u>o</u>gic." That's okay.

	1 syllable	2 syllables	3 syllables
Of	off	uften	offering
Se	Sea	Semen	Sesame
Na	Na	naked	naturelike
In	Inn	Inside	Insulin

Compound Words 5

A compound word is formed when two words join together to become a new word; for example, softball, teapot, and armchair.

Think of as many words as you can that could join onto the <u>end</u> of the given word to make a compound word.

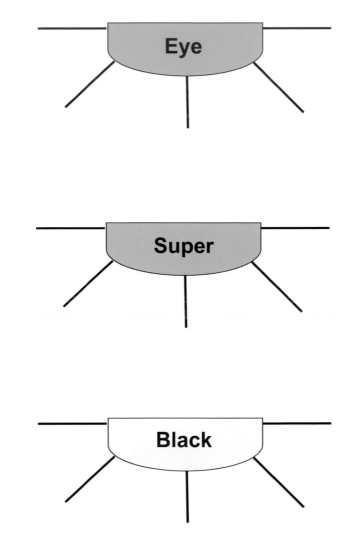

Continuous Words 5

This is a list of words joined together with the word spaces taken out. How many can you find?
Topic: ZOO ANIMALS

wolflynxlionmonkeywallabybearzebraa
ardvarkkangarooocelottigerrhinocerossn
akeelephantanteaterleopardalligatorporc
upinehyenaarmadilloostrichcheetahgira
ffegazellellamacamelgorillababoonpandab
adgerbeaverpanthercrocodilecougarbobc
atjaguarpuma

Speed Words 5

Choose words that fit the description. Use words that don't start with a capital letter, and use a different word for each question.

Choose a word that:

1	Begins with AT	
2	Has 5 letters with V in the middle	
3	Ends in SK	
4	Ends in KS	
5	Has more than 8 letters	

Concentration 5

Either underline or put a circle around all the adverbs in the passage.

Arranging an Adventure

Wilma and Wilfred thought carefully.

"What kind of adventure should we go on?" asked Wilma the Princess excitedly.

Cautiously, Wilfred the Prince replied, "A quest to find the fire-breathing dragon?"

Wilma's eyes narrowed suspiciously.

"That will be dangerous . . ."

A fire-breathing dragon wasn't what she had in mind for a handsome prince and a beautiful princess.

"I know," Wilfred replied chirpily, "dangerous but exciting!"

"Okay . . ." said Wilma slowly. "But please figure out the arrangements quickly or else I may change my mind."

Vocabulary 5

Fit the three-letter words into the correct spaces in the larger words.

HAD   **HAM**   **HOP**   **HER**   **HIM**   **HUT**

S _ _ _ P O O

S _ _ _ T E R

S _ _ _ O W

S _ _ _ P I N G

S _ _ _ M E R

S _ _ _ R Y

Change a Letter 5

Change one letter in the word so it fits the definition.

Word	Definition	New word
RICE	Well-off	
RICE	Compete	
RICE	Small animals/rodents	
WEEK	Vegetable	
WEEK	Unwanted plant	
WEEK	Not strong	
SWAM	Large water bird	
SWAM	Exchange	
SWAM	Pretend, fake	

Hat Words 5

Fill in the rows with words that end with the letter Y. Try not to use plurals.

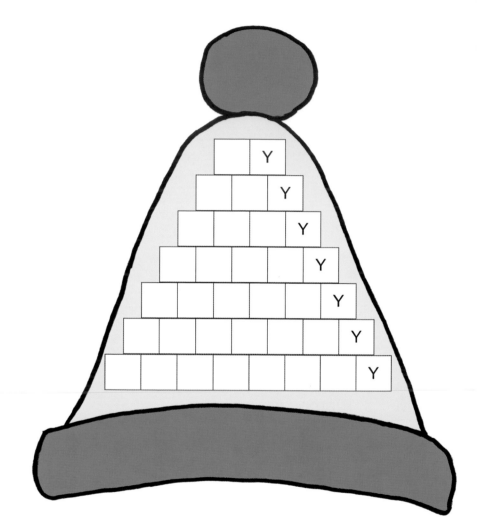

Categories 5

The list contains words that fall into three categories: adjective, adverb, and noun.
Write the words into the correct category in the balloons.

perfectly   certainly   correctly   perfect   correction

certainty   perfection   correct   certain

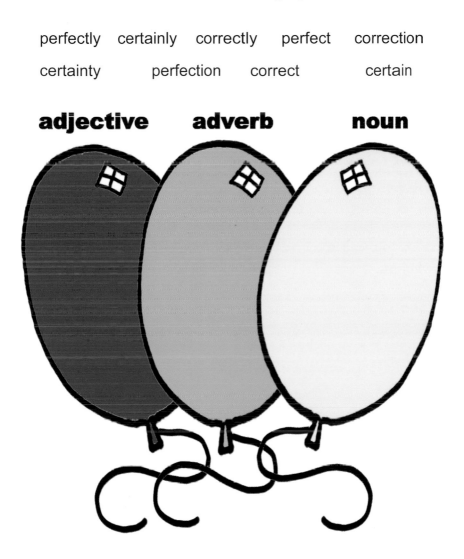

adjective   **adverb**   **noun**

Gridword 5

Place the words so they fit in the grid. A letter has been filled in for you.
There may be more than one way to do it.

ALIVE

EVENT

TERSE

TEASE

ELECT

RAISE

	■		■	
			S	
	■		■	

Lizard in a Cave 5

Each cave has an anagram of a person's name.
Today the lizard wants to go in the cave with a **girl**. Solve the
anagrams and write the words beneath the caves, then color
in or put a circle around the cave the lizard would like to go in.

How Many 5

How many words can you think of that <u>only</u> contain one vowel, the letter **U**? The letter U can be anywhere in the word.
Aim for the number stated in each column, though you can do more if you like.

Words that contain the letter U	
1 U Aim for 12	2 U's Aim for 1

Change and Rhyme 5

Change one letter in both words in the pair so they rhyme. For example, LIFT & WIRE becomes LIFE & WIFE.
There may be more than one solution.

SHARE & MAZE

BLUR & TOP

Q Crosswords 5

A straightforward crossword in the shape of a Q.

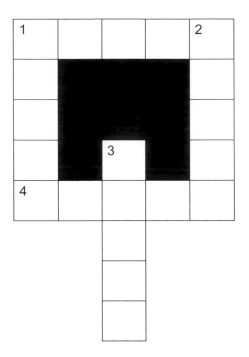

ACROSS

1. What you can also call a rabbit
4. What a bee or wasp can do

DOWN

1. Like shoes, only bigger
2. Not old
3. Striped animal

Wheel Words 5

Work out what the word in each wheel reads. The letters go in a clockwise direction, and the word can start anywhere in the wheel.

Topic: SPORTS

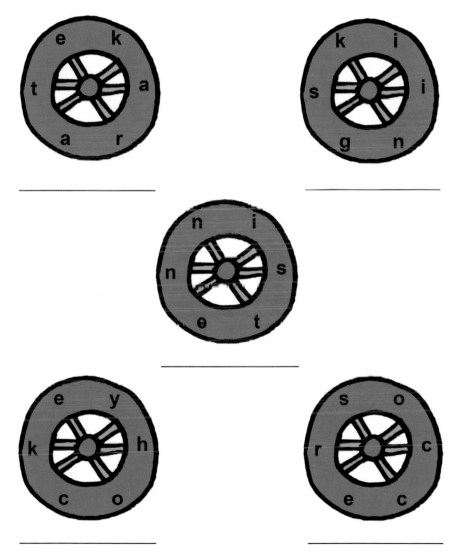

_____   _____

_____

_____   _____

Weird & Wonderful Words 5

Make a new compound word by choosing a word from each column and joining them together.
Write a description of what this new word means, and then write a sentence showing how it's used.

Snort	balloon
Cough	nest
Bumpy	idea
Ghost	bed
Dragon	ice

WORD:

DESCRIPTION:

SENTENCE:

Remove a Letter 5

Take one letter out of each word so the words make a real sentence.
For example, if you take one letter out of each of these words, PIT HIS AN WHEN, it becomes IT IS A HEN.

IS GOAT HIT MAT THEY

SMALL

AEIOU 5

The vowels A E I O U are missing from the following words. Work out which vowel goes in which word, but check carefully before you write them in!
Cross off the vowels as you use them.

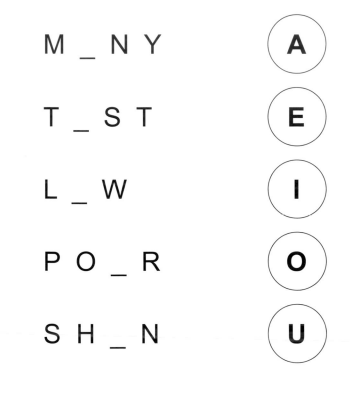

M _ N Y   (A)

T _ S T   (E)

L _ W   (I)

P O _ R   (O)

S H _ N   (U)

Skillful Sentences 5

Can you write a sentence—or sentences—with at least four words, where each word ends in the letter E?

In the Middle 5

Work out what word goes in the middle.

Three		Race
Out		Order
Wild		Chase
Frogspawn		Frog
Third		Lucky
Up		Running
Salt		City
World		Two

Level 6

Word Line 6

Start at the letter in the circle and draw a continuous line right, left, up, or down (though not diagonally) to find the letters in the saying. The punctuation marks are not included.

"The more he gave away, the more delighted he became."
The Rainbow Fish

a	g	e	h	e	h	g
v	e	h	(T)	m	t	i
e	m	e	r	o	e	l
a	a	b	e	h	d	e
w	c	e	e	m		d
a	y	t	h	o	r	e

192

Umbrella Words 6

These umbrellas have letters on them. With the umbrella closed you can only see two letters. Work out words that might be written on the umbrella when it is open. The word has to contain these two letters in this order, but it can be as long or short as you like, and the letters can appear anywhere in the word. See if you can find different ways to include the letters in a word.

Train Words 6

Can you find the three-letter words hidden in the train cars?
Put a circle around them.

ear   era   are   tea   eat   ate

Anagrams 6

Work out the anagrams, then draw a line between the words that are word pairs.

Word pairs are two words that often go together, for example, "man and wife."

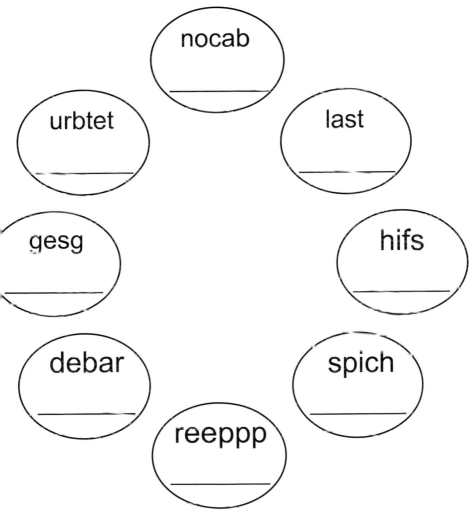

nocab
_____

urbtet
_____

last
_____

gesg
_____

hifs
_____

debar
_____

reeppp
_____

spich
_____

Alphabet Teasers 6

Choose words that fit into the grid using the letters given.

Begins with	Noun	Adjective	Verb
S			
H			
M			
L			

Fishing 6

Fish for the right letters to make words that solve the clues.

Small mammal (3)   _ _ _

Chew (3)   _ _ _

Definite article (3)   _ _ _

Have a conversation (4)   _ _ _ _

Warmth (4)   _ _ _ _

Break a rule (5)   _ _ _ _ _

Instruct (5)   _ _ _ _ _

Mini Word Sudoku 6

Write a letter from the four-letter word **"plan"** in each square so that each column, row, and mini-grid contains all the letters from the word.

		p	
n			
			l
	a		

Alphabet 6

Put a circle around the words where the letters are in reverse alphabetical order.
Use the alphabet to help you: **a b c d e f g h i j k l m n o p q r s t u v w x y z**

ton	kin	sea	ink
beg	rig	rim	red
woe	got	lie	men
urn	you	spa	tug
sly	use	she	boa

Time to Rhyme 6

In each flower, put a circle around any words in the petals that rhyme with the word in the middle. Then write another word in the empty petal that rhymes with the word in the middle and ends in the underlined letters.

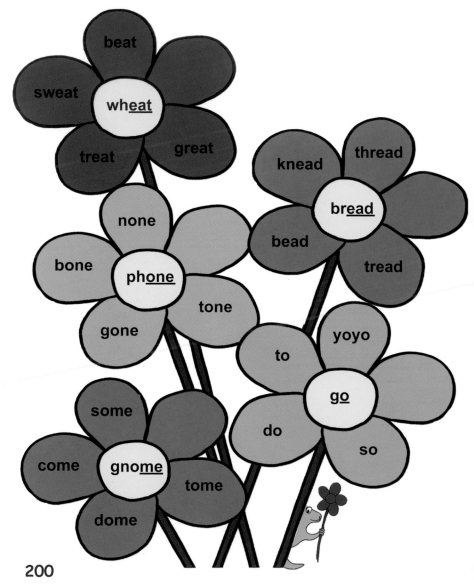

The Big X Word Search 6

The words to find are in pairs. You will find each pair of words in the shape of an X.

Can you find:
BRADY - FRANK
JIMMY - TOMÁS
VINCE - BENNY
JASON - MOSES
COSMO - BASIL

Z	A	Q	J	W	S	B	T	X	C	C
D	E	R	F	I	V	O	A	B	O	G
T	Y	H	N	M	M	J	Y	S	U	J
M	K	I	J	A	O	M	M	P	I	L
M	N	K	S	A	O	O	Y	I	J	L
F	N	B	H	B	S	U	Y	G	V	C
F	R	T	R	E	B	O	R	D	V	X
Z	S	A	S	E	W	E	N	I	A	Q
A	D	Z	N	X	S	W	N	E	D	C
Y	V	F	R	K	T	C	G	N	B	N
H	Y	U	J	M	E	K	I	L	Y	O

The Word Store 6

The Word Store is a special place that sells different kinds of words. Today we are going shopping for **nouns** (person, place, or thing). Wherever there is a space in the story, write in a noun that starts with the letter given. It's a good idea to read through the story first to get a feel for what you may want to write. If you write in pencil, you can do the puzzle more than once and make the story different each time.

The Word Store

Mark looked at the big pile of

b _____ on the floor

and thought ,"However am I going

to find my d_____?"

His f _____ had

knocked them off the shelf when looking for his

c _____.

He didn't find it, but did find a m _____ and a

p _____ that had been hidden for a while.

"I'll buy a new one," thought Mark. On his way to the

store he met Marie, his neighbor, who had a new

p _____ AND a new t _____!

Mark was surprised. Marie was OLD and old people

didn't have those kinds of things! He expected

her to buy things like h_____ and

g_____.

Letters 6

Color the squares with **capital letters** in **yellow**.
Color the squares with **lower case letters** in **purple**.
Then work out what the picture is.

m	c	h	D	k	t	f	J	b	y	p	B
y	D	L	F	z	T	c	E	H	h	F	T
h	z	p	Z	b	m	k	Y	C	p	Y	P
f	H	L	K	Y	C	f	N	K	K	L	N
b	t	k	B	h	J	p	F	D	m	Z	H

Words and Sounds 6

Homonyms are words that are spelled and pronounced the same but have different meanings. Use the word in the balloon to make up a sentence or sentences where the word is used twice with two different meanings.
The first one has been done for you.

I heard my dog bark, then scratch at the bark on the tree.

Synonyms 6

A synonym is a word that means exactly or nearly the same as another word; for example, "sad" and "unhappy" are synonyms. Find the pairs of synonyms and draw a line connecting the two.

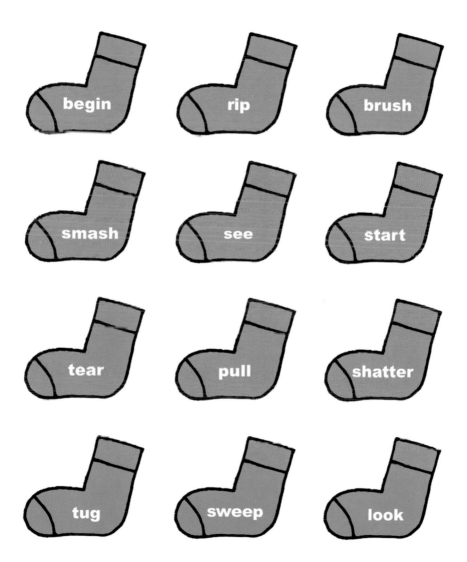

Acronyms 6

Acronyms are words formed from the initial letters of other words. For example, **ASPS** could stand for "American Society Protecting Snakes."

Work out what the three acronyms could stand for, then make up one of your own at the end.

Theme: COMICS

Definitions 6

Choose the correct definition for each word.

Kimono	1) Japanese relatives 2) Japanese drink 3) Japanese robe
Hygiene	1) A plant 2) Keeping clean and healthy 3) Medicine
Quiff	1) Curl of hair on forehead 2) Feather used for writing 3) Drunk
Lyre	1) One who does not tell the truth 2) Instrument like a harp 3) Poem
Hostile	1) Unfriendly 2) A house for students 3) To push roughly

Leaping Lizard 6

The words of a sentence have been jumbled up and placed onto rocks. The lizard is sitting by the rock with the first word. Work out which order the words go in, and draw a line to show the lizard which way to jump.

You can write the sentence at the bottom.

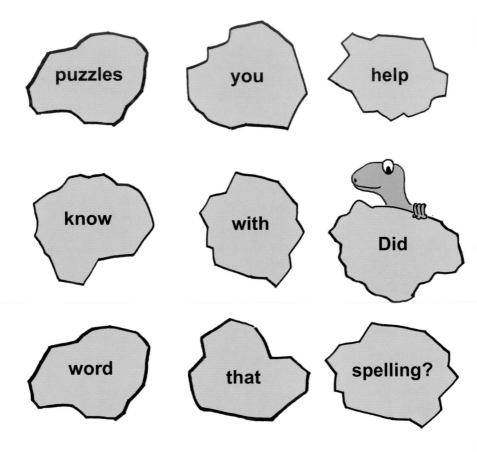

Sentence: _____

Syllables 6

Add a letter or letters to the ones already given to make words that are 1, 2, and 3 syllables long.

Note that the sound of the vowel may change; for example, "l<u>o</u>w" and "l<u>o</u>gic." That's okay.

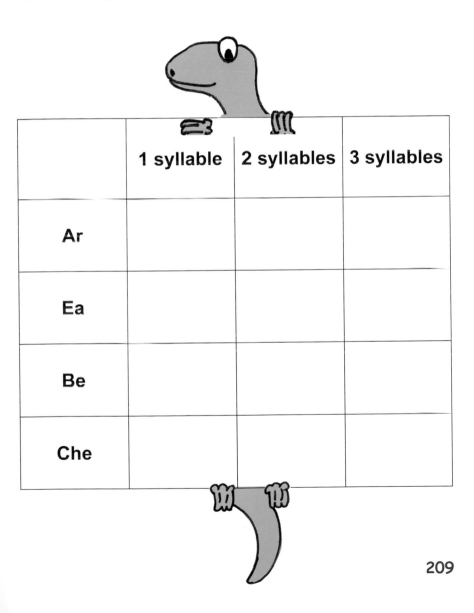

	1 syllable	2 syllables	3 syllables
Ar			
Ea			
Be			
Che			

Compound Words 6

A compound word is formed when two words join together to become a new word; for example, softball, teapot, and armchair.

Think of as many words as you can that could join onto the <u>end</u> of the given word to make a compound word.

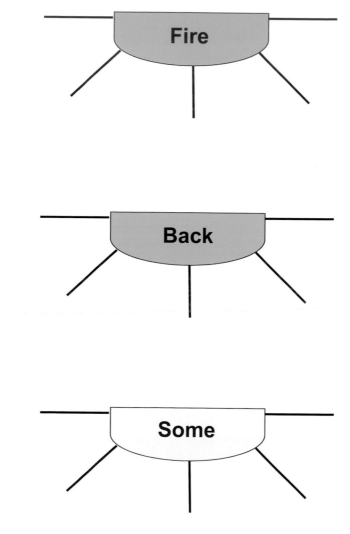

Continuous Words 6

This is a list of words joined together with the word spaces taken out. How many can you find?
Topic: JOBS

judgecoachnurseeditorprofessordoctorpilo
tpoetteacherbarberbakerbrokeractorfarm
ermechanicchauffeurcheffirefighterpharm
acistdentisttailorsoldierprinterwaiterwatchm
akerathleteaccountantveterinarianbeautic
ianbankeractresssalesmanmagicianmusici
anauthorsailorpolicemanpoliticiancarpente
rengineerfishermancraftsmanwaitressbu
tchershoemakerlawyer

Speed Words 6

Choose words that fit the description. Use words that don't start with a capital letter, and use a different word for each question.

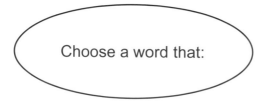

Choose a word that:

1	Has 3 letters, all of which are in alphabetical order	
2	Has 2 G's but not together	
3	Is an anagram of E M S U O	
4	Fits into __ __ X __ __	
5	Is a palindrome (reads the same forwards and backwards)	

Concentration 6

Put a circle around all the comparatives and superlatives in the passage. (Example: the comparative of the word "happy" is "happier," and the superlative is "happiest.")

Wilma and Wilfred on an Adventure

It wasn't the best trip that Wilma had ever been on. Climbing the rocky mountains was harder than she expected, and crossing shark-infested rivers was definitely the worst part.

"Meeting a fire-breathing dragon will be easier than this," she grumbled as she waded through the river, her princess dress getting wetter and messier.

Wilfred, however, was feeling more excited with each step he took.

"We're getting nearer to the dragon!" he shouted excitedly. "I can see the biggest dragon flames I've ever seen!"

Wilma sighed. This wasn't the princess-type adventure she had hoped for.

Vocabulary 6

Fit the three-letter words into the correct spaces in the larger words.

ASS ARM AMP EAR ELM ONE

H _ _ _ E T

H _ _ _ O N Y

H _ _ _ L E

H _ _ _ S T

H _ _ _ T H

H _ _ _ E R

Change a Letter 6

Change one letter in the word so it fits the definition.

Word	Definition	New word
NOSE	Musical sound	
NOSE	Got up	
NOSE	Inquisitive/wanting to know	
OVEN	Not odd	
OVEN	Not closed	
OVEN	Above	
DATE	Opening in fence	
DATE	Have courage	
DATE	Information/facts	

Hat Words 6

Fill in the rows with words that end with the letter E. Try not to use plurals.

Categories 6

The list contains words that fall into two categories: adjectives generally used to describe people, and adjectives generally used to describe animals.
Write the words into the correct category in the balloons.

humorous   tame   charming   scaly   confident

ferocious   creative   playful   successful   poisonous

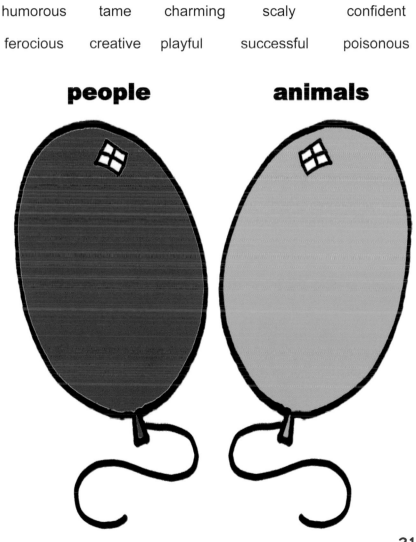

people   **animals**

Gridword 6

Place the words so they fit in the grid. Two letters have been filled in for you.
There may be more than one way to do it.

CAMEL

CAROL

COLIC

COMIC

LINER

MINIM

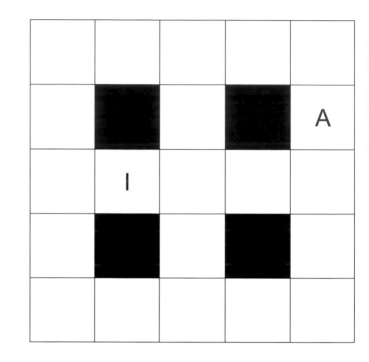

Lizard in a Cave 6

Each cave has an anagram of a creature.
Today the lizard wants to go in the cave with a creature that is **small**. Solve the anagrams and write the words beneath the caves, then color in or put a circle around the cave the lizard would like to go in.

P H I O P

_____

H O N I R

_____

L E A H W

_____

S U M O E

_____

B A R E Z

_____

How Many 6

How many words can you think of that contain the letter **S**? There can be any other vowels and consonants in the word, and the letter S can come anywhere.

Aim for the number stated in each column, though you can do more if you like.

Words that contain the letter **S**	
2 S's Aim for 12	3 or more S's Aim for 1

Change and Rhyme 6

Change one letter in both words in the pair so they rhyme. For example, LIFT & WIRE becomes LIFE & WIFE.
There may be more than one solution.

LEAD & ROAR

HERD & VERY

Q Crosswords 6

A straightforward crossword in the shape of a Q.

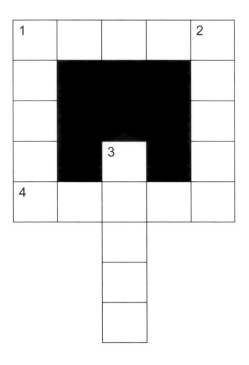

ACROSS
1. One of the colors of the American flag
4. Mistake

DOWN
1. Very large sea creature
2. To go in
3. Water, coffee, and juice are examples of this

Wheel Words 6

Work out what the word in each wheel reads. The letters go in <u>either direction</u>, and the word can start anywhere in the wheel.
Topic: TYPES OF BUILDINGS

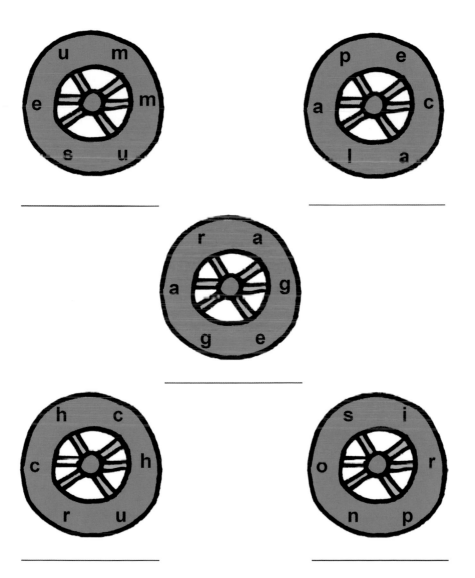

Weird & Wonderful Words 6

Make a new compound word by choosing a word from each column and joining them together.
Write a description of what this new word means, and then write a sentence showing how it's used.

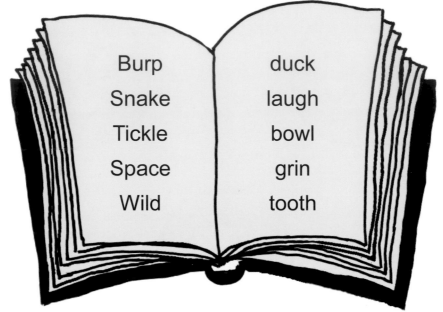

Burp	duck
Snake	laugh
Tickle	bowl
Space	grin
Wild	tooth

WORD:

DESCRIPTION:

SENTENCE:

Remove a Letter 6

Take one letter out of each word so the words make a real sentence.
For example, if you take one letter out of each of these words, PIT HIS AN WHEN, it becomes IT IS A HEN.

FLOUR PLUSH FLOUR HIS

WEIGHT

A E I O U 6

The vowels A E I O U are missing from the following words. Work out which vowel goes in which word, but check carefully before you write them in!
Cross off the vowels as you use them.

W _ F E   **A**

B _ K E   **E**

S _ A K   **I**

F L _ N G   **O**

S H _ L L   **U**

Skillful Sentences 6

Can you write a sentence—or sentences—with at least four words, where none of the words contain the letter E?

Level 7

Word Line 7

Start at the letter in the circle and draw a continuous line right, left, up, or down (though not diagonally) to find the letters in the saying. The punctuation marks are not included.

"It does not do to dwell on dreams and forget to live."
Harry Potter

d	o	t	o	l	o	n
t		e	d	l	r	d
o	n	v	w	e	e	a
e	s	i	l	o	f	m
o	(l)	t	o	r	d	s
d	t	t	e	g	n	a

Umbrella Words 7

These umbrellas have letters on them. With the umbrella closed you can only see two letters. Work out words that might be written on the umbrella when it is open. The word has to contain these two letters in this order, but it can be as long or short as you like, and the letters can appear anywhere in the word. See if you can find different ways to include the letters in a word.

w e

b i

f f

t h

Train Words 7

Can you find the three-letter words hidden in the train cars?
Now they get a bit harder!

ray   bar   bay   pay   yap   rap

Anagrams 7

Work out the anagrams, then draw a line between the words that are word pairs.

Word pairs are two words that often go together; for example, "man and wife."

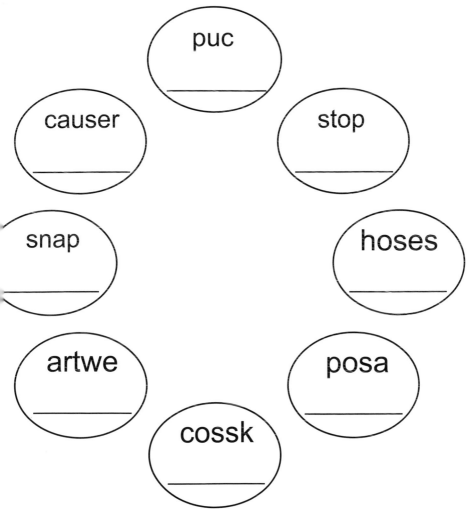

Alphabet Teasers 7

Choose words that fit into the grid using the letters given.

Begins with	Noun	Adjective	Verb
D			
V			
J			
T			

Fishing 7

Fish for the right letters to make words that solve the clues.

Male child (3)   __ __ __

Frozen liquid (3)   __ __ __

Money (4)   __ __ __ __

One time (4)   __ __ __ __

Pleasant (4)   __ __ __ __

From a past time till now (5)   __ __ __ __ __

A sound (5)   __ __ __ __ __

Mini Word Sudoku 7

Place the letters from the six-letter word **"brainy"** in the grid so that each column, each row, and each of the six 2×3 sub-grids contains all the six letters from the word.

a					i
	r	y	n	b	
r	y	i	a	n	b
b					r
	i	b	r	a	
y					n

Alphabet 7

Put a circle around the words where the all the letters are from the first half of the alphabet.

Use the alphabet to help you: **a b c d e f g h i j k l m n o p q r s t u v w x y z**

milk   lock   mink   glee

golf   hand   jak   dust

moon   fall   brim   able

wait   made   lime   near

break   rust   boom   chef

Time to Rhyme 7

In each flower, put a circle around any words in the petals that rhyme with the word in the middle. Then write another word in the empty petal that rhymes with the word in the middle and ends in the underlined letters.

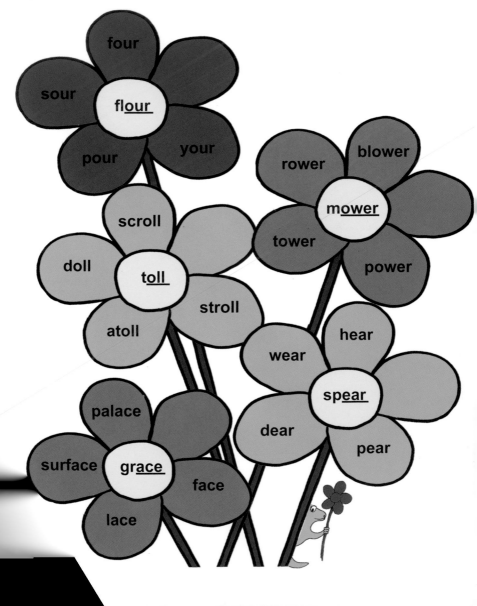

The Big X Word Search 7

The words to find are in pairs. You will find each pair of names in the shape of an X.

Can you find:
JULIE - DELIA
ELENA - IRENA
MOIRA - TRISH
JANET - ANNIE
CAROL - LORNA

Q	E	E	Y	I	I	J	P	S	F	A
H	K	L	Z	R	C	N	A	B	N	M
W	E	Q	E	R	Y	T	U	N	O	I
P	S	N	A	N	D	G	I	F	E	H
J	A	J	L	D	A	E	K	Z	C	T
X	U	V	E	N	B	C	M	Q	E	L
W	T	L	R	Y	M	T	A	U	O	I
O	I	R	I	O	P	S	A	R	F	H
A	G	J	I	E	L	K	N	Z	O	C
X	V	R	N	S	B	A	N	M	Q	L
F	A	H	K	Z	H	C	B	M	W	T

The Word Store 7

The Word Store is a special place that sells different kinds of words. Today we are going shopping for **verbs** (action words). Wherever there is a space in the story, write in a verb that starts with the letter given. It's a good idea to read through the story first to get a feel for what you may want to write. If you write in pencil, you can do the puzzle more than once and make the story different each time.

The Word Store

Eddie liked to s _____,

while his sister Dora liked to

d _____. Sometimes they

would p _____ together.

"Please don't b _____

your mother today," said Dad. "Just go outside and

p _____."

Eddie and Dora g _____.

Dora looked at Eddie and s _____.

Eddie looked at Dora and said, "Let's a _____

Mom and Dad!"

So they j _____ and r_____

and l_____, but they didn't want to

s _____ in case they got in trouble.

Letters 7

Color the squares with **the letter p** in **red**.
Color the squares with **the letter b** in **yellow**.
Color the squares with **the letter d** in **blue**.
Then work out what the picture is.

p	b	d	d	d	h	p	b	p	b	h	p
p	b	p	h	d	h	d	b	p	b	p	b
d	b	d	b	d	b	p	p	p	b	b	p
p	b	d	p	d	b	p	h	p	b	p	p
b	b	d	d	d	b	p	h	p	b	p	h
b	b	d	d	d	h	p	p	p	h	b	h

Words and Sounds 7

Homonyms are words that are spelled and pronounced the same but have different meanings. Use the word in the balloon to make up a sentence or sentences where the word is used twice with two different meanings.

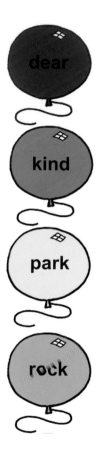

Synonyms 7

A synonym is a word that means exactly or nearly the same as another word; for example, "sad" and "unhappy" are synonyms. Find the pairs of synonyms and draw a line connecting the two.

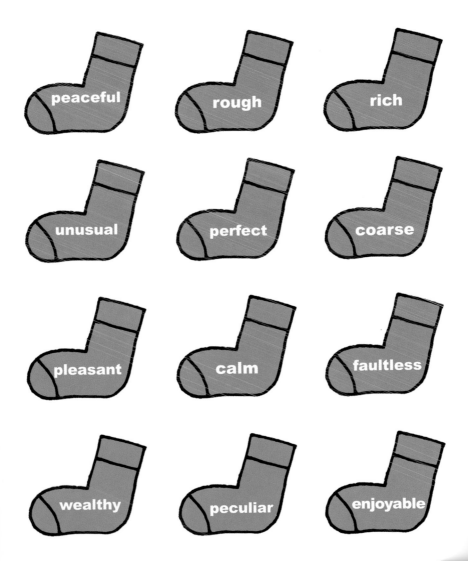

Acronyms 7

Acronyms are words formed from the initial letters of other words. For example, **ASPS** could stand for "American Society Protecting Snakes."

Work out what the three acronyms could stand for, then make up one of your own at the end.

Theme: TECHNOLOGY

Definitions 7

Choose the correct definition for each word.

Umpteen	1)	A lot
	2)	Young teenager
	3)	Small umbrella
Consequence	1)	A discussion
	2)	A list of numbers
	3)	What happens as a result
Quaint	1)	Bird like a partridge
	2)	Dainty, old fashioned
	3)	Quarter of a gallon
Jovial	1)	Youngster
	2)	Another name for Jupiter
	3)	Merry, good humored
Nettle	1)	Stinging plant
	2)	To settle comfortably
	3)	The lower part

Leaping Lizard 7

The words of a sentence have been jumbled up and placed onto rocks. The lizard is sitting by the rock with the first word. Work out which order the words go in, and draw a line to show the lizard which way to jump.
You can write the sentence at the bottom.

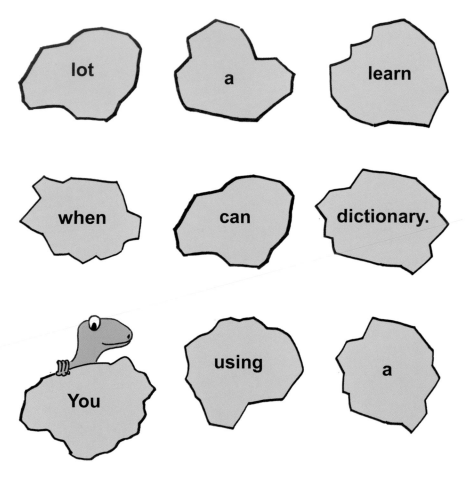

Sentence: _____

Syllables 7

Add a letter or letters to the ones already given to make words that are 1, 2, and 3 syllables long.
Note that the sound of the vowel may change; for example, "l<u>ow</u>" and "l<u>o</u>gic." That's okay.

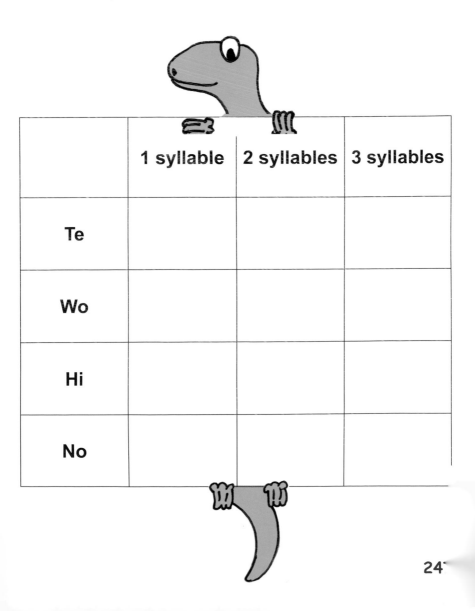

	1 syllable	2 syllables	3 syllables
Te			
Wo			
Hi			
No			

Compound Words 7

A compound word is formed when two words join together to become a new word; for example, softball, teapot, and armchair.

Think of as many words as you can that could join onto the <u>beginning</u> of the given word to make a compound word.

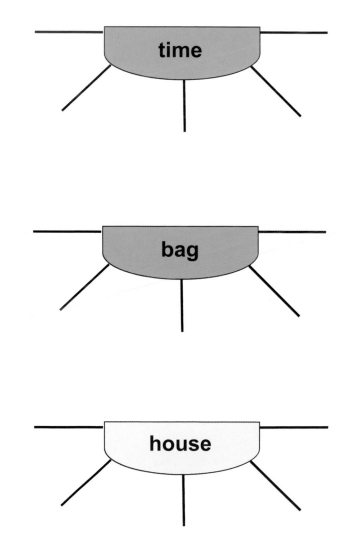

Continuous Words 7

This is a list of words joined together with the word spaces taken out. How many can you find?
Topic: WORDS CONTAINING "SH"

**shipwishdishshedshiftfishpushshutblu
shshrubcashclashsharerashharshfreshm
arshshamesheepshopshowposhbrushbush**

Speed Words 7

Choose words that fit the description. Use words that don't start with a capital letter, and use a different word for each question.

Choose a word that:

1	Rhymes with HEATER	
2	Has no vowels	
3	Includes 2 R's	
4	Has 2 syllables and starts with Q	
5	Has 2 syllables and ends with W	

Concentration 7

Read the passage and answer the questions at the end.

The Dragon

"RAARGH!!" roared the dragon as Wilma and Wilfred approached it. "I am a dragon who breathes fire, and you will be sizzled like a sausage. RAARGH!"

Wilfred raised an eyebrow.

"That's not a very pleasant greeting," he scolded. "Perhaps 'Hello, how are you?' would be more polite?"

"Oh, sorry," said the dragon. "Let me start again. Welcome to my cave. Would you like a cup of tea?"

"Thank you," replied Wilfred and Wilma. "That would be lovely."

QUESTIONS

1. How many words have 2 letters? _____

2. How many words have 2 syllables? _____

Vocabulary 7

Fit the three-letter words into the correct spaces in the larger words.

RAG   RAM   RAN   RAP   RAW   RIB   RUM

D _ _ _ A T I C

D _ _ _ O N

D _ _ _ M E R

D _ _ _ E R

D _ _ _ B L E

D _ _ _ E S

D _ _ _ K

Change a Letter 7

Change one letter in the word so it fits the definition.

Word	Definition	New word
DAME	Moist, wet	
DAME	Rounded roof	
DOUR	Opening	
DOUR	Has an acidic taste	
EARS	Vehicles	
EARS	Obtain income/money	
EASE	Direction	
EASE	Container for flowers	
DULY	Ought to do	
DULY	Boring	

Hat Words 7

Fill in the rows with words that begin with the letter W. Try not to use plurals.

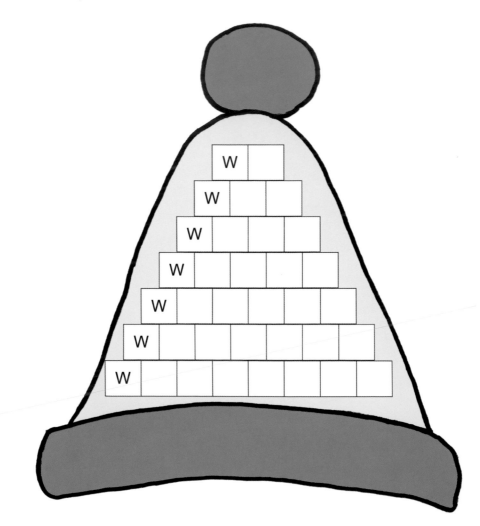

Categories 7

The list contains words that fall into three categories: countries in South America, countries in Europe, and countries in Africa. Write the words into the correct category in the balloons.

Argentina   Spain   Brazil   Uganda   France

Peru   Germany   Nigeria   Kenya

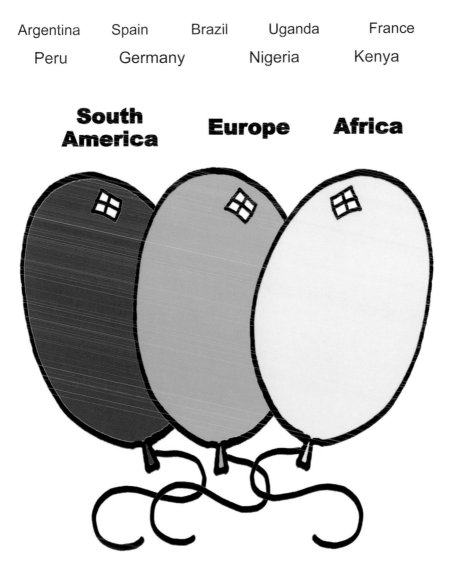

South America

Europe

Africa

Gridword 7

Place the words so they fit in the grid. A letter has been filled in for you.
There may be more than one way to do it.

MERITS

SITTER

THESIS

ASSERT

SHEETS

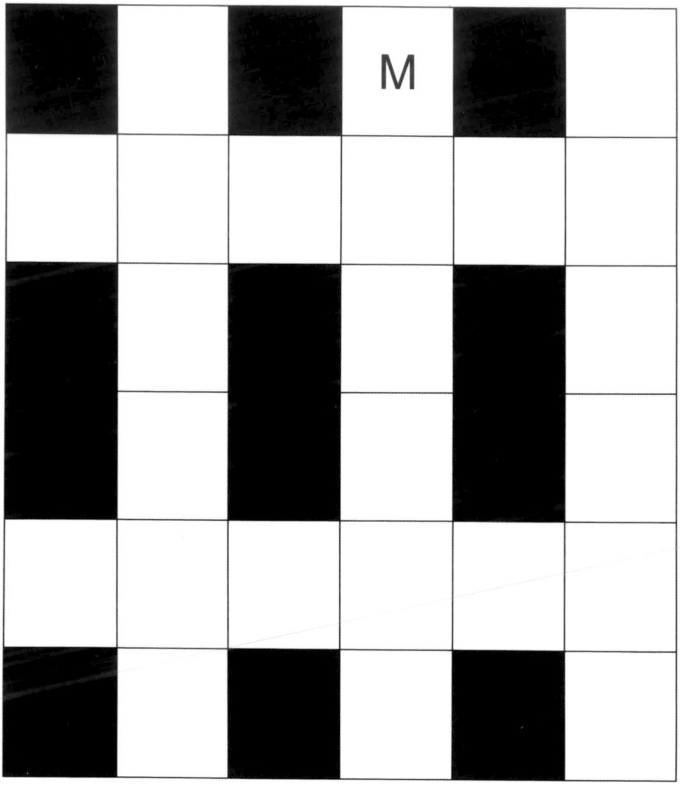

Lizard in a Cave 7

Each cave has an anagram of a type of food.
Today the lizard wants to go in the cave with a **vegetable**.
Solve the anagrams and write the words beneath the caves,
then color in or put a circle around the cave the lizard would
like to go in.

How Many 7

How many words can you think of that contain the letter L?
There can be any other vowels and consonants in the word,
and the letter L can come anywhere.
Aim for the number stated in each column, though you can do
more if you like.

Words that contain the letter **L**	
2 L's Aim for 12	3 or more L's Aim for 1

Change and Rhyme 7

Change one letter in both words in the pair so they rhyme. For
example, LIFT & WIRE becomes LIFE & WIFE.
There may be more than one solution.

TOUGH & MUCK

HOUR & CORN

Q Crosswords 7

A straightforward crossword in the shape of a Q.

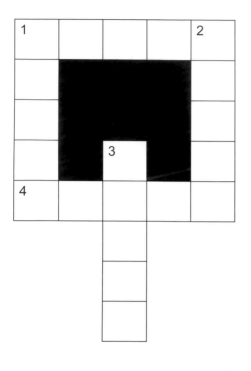

ACROSS

1. You may add it to tea or coffee
4. One of the colors of the rainbow

DOWN

1. You may find it in a child's playground
2. A bird often seen in winter
3. A number

Wheel Words 7

Work out what the word in each wheel reads. The letters go in <u>either direction</u>, and the word can start anywhere in the wheel.
Topic: HOUSEHOLD ITEMS

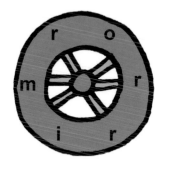

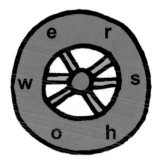

_____

_____

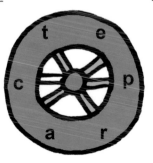

_____

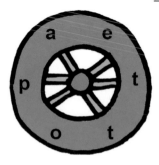

_____

_____

Weird & Wonderful Words 7

Make a new compound word by choosing a word from each column and joining them together.
Write a description of what this new word means, and then write a sentence showing how it's used.

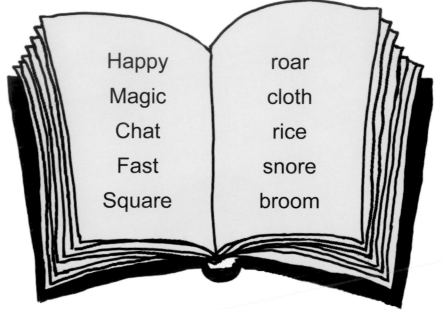

Happy	roar
Magic	cloth
Chat	rice
Fast	snore
Square	broom

WORD:

DESCRIPTION:

SENTENCE:

Remove a Letter 7

Take one letter out of each word so the words make a real sentence.
For example, if you take one letter out of each of these words, PIT HIS AN WHEN, it becomes IT IS A HEN.

THEN STUN HIS SETTLING

A E I O U 7

The vowels A E I O U are missing from the following words. Work out which vowel goes in which word, but check carefully before you write them in!
Cross off the vowels as you use them.

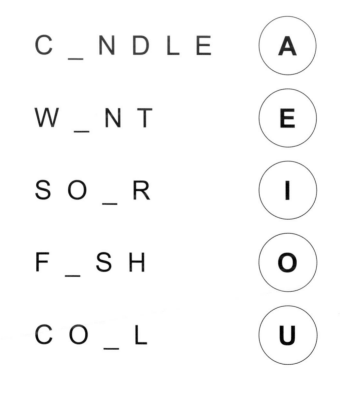

C _ N D L E   (A)

W _ N T   (E)

S O _ R   (I)

F _ S H   (O)

C O _ L   (U)

Skillful Sentences 7

Can you write a sentence—or sentences—with at least four words, that contains at least one palindrome?
A palindrome is a word that reads the same backwards as forwards; for example, the word "nun."

Level 8

Word Line 8

Start at the letter in the circle and draw a continuous line right, left, up, or down (though not diagonally) to find the letters in the saying. The punctuation marks are not included.

"No act of kindness, no matter how small, is ever wasted."
Aesop

r	e	t	t	a	m	t	c	Ⓝ
h	l	i	s	e	o	o	a	o
o	l	t	e	v	n	f	k	i
w	a	s	d	e	s	s	e	n
s	m	a	w	r			n	d

Umbrella Words 8

These umbrellas have letters on them. With the umbrella closed you can only see two letters. Work out words that might be written on the umbrella when it is open. The word has to contain these two letters in this order, but it can be as long or short as you like, and the letters can appear anywhere in the word. See if you can find different ways to include the letters in a word.

Train Words 8

Can you find the three-letter words hidden in the train cars?

lag   leg   gel   gal   lea   ale

Anagrams 8

Work out the anagrams, then draw a line between the words that are word pairs.

Word pairs are two words that often go together; for example, "man and wife."

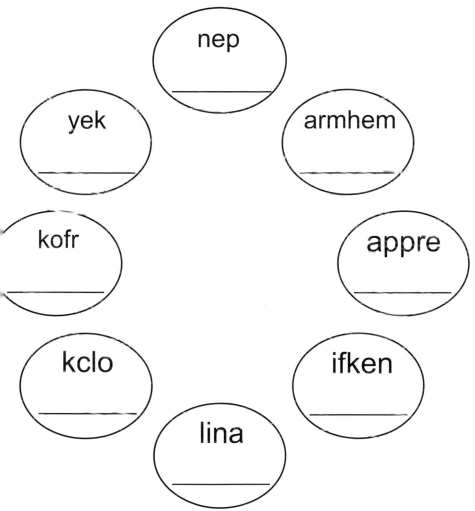

Alphabet Teasers 8

Choose words that fit into the grid using the letters given.

Begins with	Noun	Adjective	Verb
I			
K			
W			
Y			

Fishing 8

Fish for the right letters to make words that solve the clues.

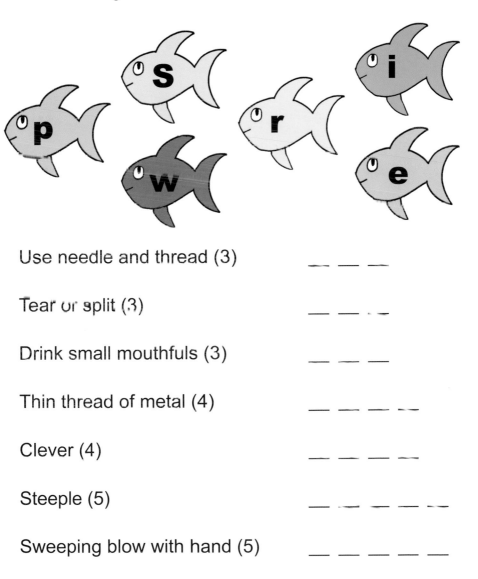

Use needle and thread (3)   __ __ __

Tear or split (3)   __ __ __

Drink small mouthfuls (3)   __ __ __

Thin thread of metal (4)   __ __ __ __

Clever (4)   __ __ __ __

Steeple (5)   __ __ __ __ __

Sweeping blow with hand (5)   __ __ __ __ __

Mini Word Sudoku 8

Place the letters from the six-letter word **"signal"** in the grid so that each column, each row, and each of the six 2×3 subgrids contains all of the six letters from the word.

	a				s
		n	l		
n				a	
s					n
	n	g			
	l		i	n	

Alphabet 8

Put a circle around the words where the all of the letters are from the second half of the alphabet.
Use the alphabet to help you: **a b c d e f g h i j k l m n o p q r s t u v w x y z**

quote	strum	story	torn
pour	oxen	worst	lost
stolen	rusty	trout	young
swoop	zoom	quip	potty
worry	shout	nouns	thrust

Time to Rhyme 8

In each flower, put a circle around any words in the petals that rhyme with the word in the middle. Then write another word in the empty petal that rhymes with the word in the middle and ends in the underlined letters.

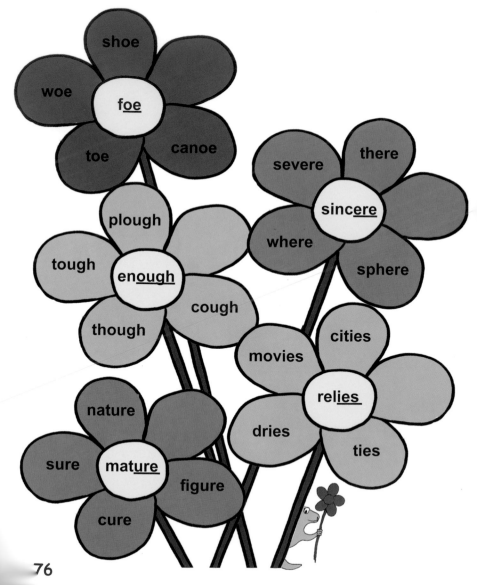

The Big X Word Search 8

The words to find are in pairs. You will find each pair of names in the shape of an X.

Can you find:
LINDA - BUNTY
MARIE - CARLA
DEBBY - MABEL
ELISE - HEIDI
GRACE - CIARA

F	R	Y	S	N	C	M	Q	H	G	K
M	L	S	D	C	D	I	M	R	F	G
H	A	J	A	E	K	A	A	L	Z	X
C	V	R	B	N	B	C	M	R	L	K
W	L	E	I	E	E	B	R	T	A	Y
A	U	I	L	E	E	O	Y	P	H	O
B	I	Y	T	L	R	L	E	E	W	Q
A	U	S	I	D	F	G	I	H	J	K
L	K	N	G	A	S	D	M	S	N	B
B	D	V	T	C	I	X	Z	A	E	S
A	E	T	R	Y	U	U	I	B	S	B

The Word Store 8

The Word Store is a special place that sells different kinds of words. Today we are going shopping for **verbs** (action words). Wherever there is a space in the story, write in a verb that starts with the letter given. It's a good idea to read through the story first to get a feel for what you may want to write. If you write in pencil, you can do the puzzle more than once and make the story different each time.

Kira s _____ at the box.

"Yes, please o _____ it," she said. "But don't d _____ it."

Jordan q _____ her.

"Are you sure? I can h _____ it and c _____ it if you'd like me to?"

Kira t_____.

"No, don't t _____. It may b _____ if you do that."

Jordan w _____ to s _____ it.

"Stop!" Kira y _____.

"P_____ it down!"

Letters 8

Color the squares with **the letter M** in **green**.
Color the squares with **the letter W** in **purple**.
Then work out what the picture is.

M	M	M	M	M	M	M	M	M	M
W	W	W	W	W	W	W	W	W	M
M	M	M	M	M	M	M	M	W	M
M	W	W	W	W	W	W	M	W	M
M	W	M	M	M	M	W	M	W	M
M	W	M	W	W	M	W	M	W	M
M	W	M	W	W	W	W	M	W	M
M	W	M	M	M	M	M	M	W	M
M	W	W	W	W	W	W	W	W	M
M	M	M	M	M	M	M	M	M	M

Words and Sounds 8

Homonyms are words that are spelled and pronounced the same but have different meanings. Use the word in the balloon to make up a sentence or sentences where the word is used twice with two different meanings.

row

tie

trip

wave

watch

Synonyms 8

A synonym is a word that means exactly or nearly the same as another word; for example, "sad" and "unhappy" are synonyms. Find the pairs of synonyms and draw a line connecting the two.

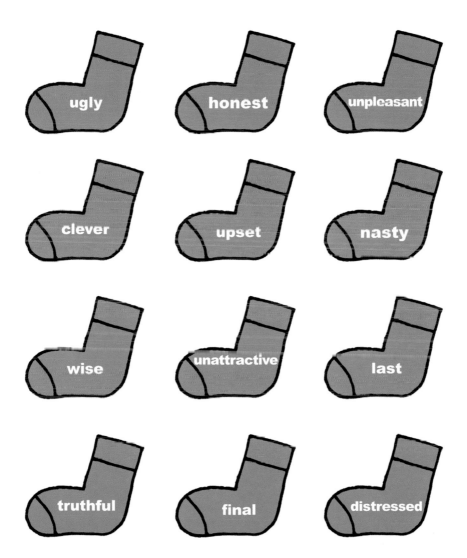

Acronyms 8

Acronyms are words formed from the initial letters of other words. For example, **ASPS** could stand for "American Society Protecting Snakes."

Work out what the three acronyms could stand for, then make up one of your own at the end.

Theme: COSTUMES AND OUTFITS

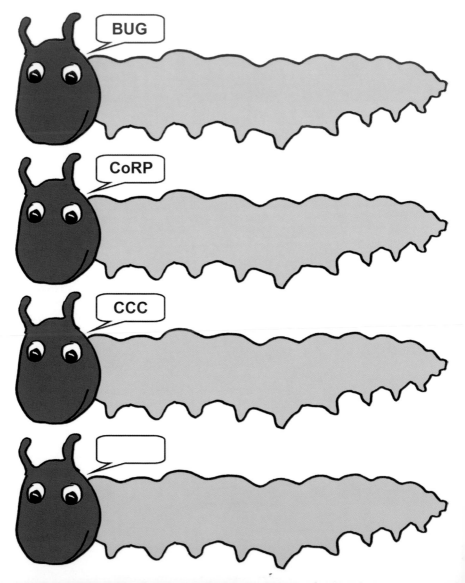

Definitions 8

Choose the correct definition for each word.

Armadillo	1) Metal clothing 2) A castle 3) An animal with a hard back
Kilt	1) Small metal pot for cooking 2) Skirt made of tartan cloth 3) In good working order
Erase	1) Rub out, delete 2) Avoid 3) Build
Treble	1) Shake with fear 2) Three times as many 3) To disturb
Yodel	1) Person who lives in the countryside 2) Person who practices yoga 3) Singing of people who live in the Swiss mountains

Leaping Lizard 8

The words of a sentence have been jumbled up and placed onto rocks. The lizard is sitting by the rock with the first word. Work out which order the words go in, and draw a line to show the lizard which way to jump.

You can write the sentence at the bottom.

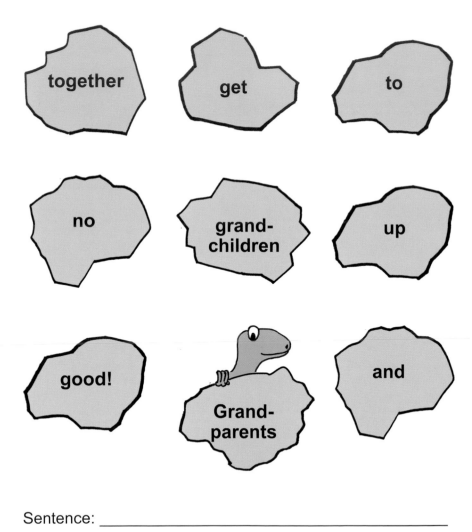

Sentence: _____

Syllables 8

Add a letter or letters to the ones already given to make words that are 1, 2, and 3 syllables long.
Note that the sound of the vowel may change; for example, "l<u>o</u>w" and "l<u>o</u>gic." That's okay.

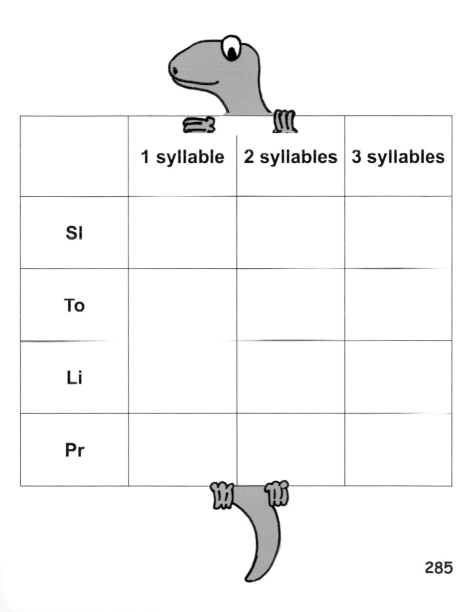

	1 syllable	2 syllables	3 syllables
Sl			
To			
Li			
Pr			

Compound Words 8

A compound word is formed when two words join together to become a new word; for example, softball, teapot, and armchair.

Think of as many words as you can that could join onto the <u>beginning</u> of the given word to make a compound word.

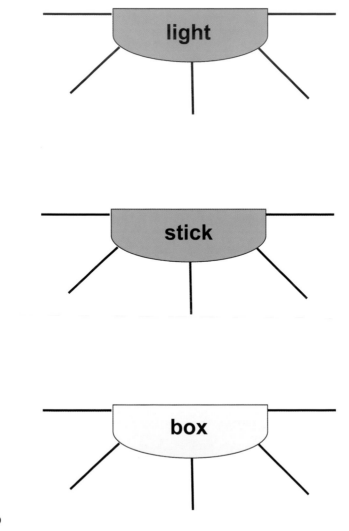

Continuous Words 8

This is a list of words joined together with the word spaces taken out. How many can you find?
Topic: WORDS CONTAINING Z

pizzazappuzzlezerozoommazezonenuzz lezebradazzledazequizzanyhazewhizzzin ggrizzlebuzzardquartzjazzwaltzlaze

Speed Words 8

Choose words that fit the description. Use words that don't start with a capital letter, and use a different word for each question.

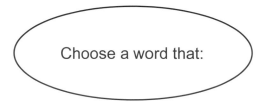

Choose a word that:

1	Has 4 letters and ends with a double letter	
2	Has 5 letters, including 3 vowels	
3	Starts with M and contains a G in the body of the word	
4	Fits into __ B __ __ T	
5	Rhymes with QUART	

Concentration 8

Read the passage and answer the questions at the end.

A Conversation with Rex

After a cup of tea and a meal of sausages and toast, personally cooked by Rex the dragon, Wilma and Wilfred explained what they wanted.

"We would like a guided tour of the places fire-breathing dragons go, please."

"Certainly," said Rex, "but you have to promise me one thing. Everyone thinks I am a scary dragon, so you have to act scary, too. Let me hear your scary voices."

"Grrr," growled Wilfred.

"Uurgh," mumbled Wilma.

Rex rolled his eyes. "Oh well, better than nothing. Let's go."

QUESTIONS

1. How many words contain 3 vowels? _____

2. How many plurals are there? _____

Vocabulary 8

Fit the three-letter words into the correct spaces in the larger words.

ADD   RAN   RAP   RIG   AGO   EEK   HIM

W __ __ __ P E D

W __ __ __ N

W __ __ __ L E

W __ __ __ P E R

W __ __ __ G L E

W __ __ __ L Y

W __ __ __ G L E

Change a Letter 8

Change one letter in the word so it fits the definition.

Word	Definition	New word
SEEM	Stalk	
SEEM	Look for	
SHOW	Frozen ice crystals	
SHOW	Foot covering	
SUET	Piece of music for two	
SUET	Clothing	
ROAR	Street	
ROAR	Space behind	
PATH	Meat paste	
PATH	Tub	

Hat Words 8

Fill in the rows with words that include the letter O. Try not to use plurals.

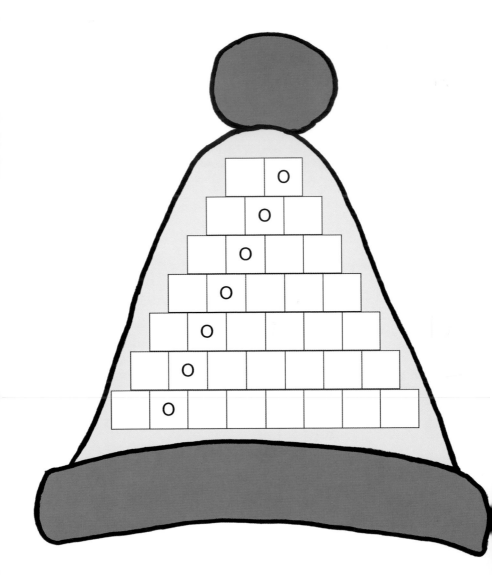

Categories 8

The list contains words that fall into two categories: American spelling and British spelling.
Write the words into the correct category in the balloons.

| ax | armour | color | grey | metre | behavior |
| axe | armor | colour | gray | meter | behaviour |

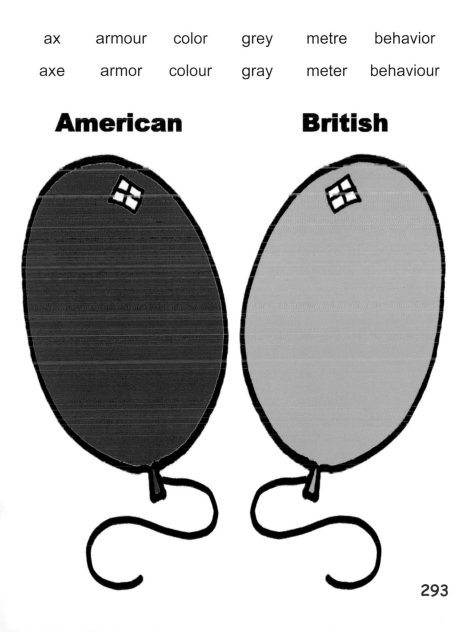

American

British

Gridword 8

Place the words so they fit in the grid. Two letters have been filled in for you.

PELLET
RECENT
SCREEN
WHENCE
CHEESE

	W		P		R
C	H	E	E	S	E
	E		L		C
	N		L		E
S	C	R	E	E	N
	E		T		T

Lizard in a Cave 8

Each cave has an anagram of a pastime.
Today the lizard wants to go in the cave with **something to read**. Solve the anagrams and write the words beneath the caves, then color in or put a circle around the cave the lizard would like to go in.

How Many 8

How many words can you think of that contain the letter **T**? There can be any other vowels and consonants in the word, and the letter T can come anywhere.

Aim for the number stated in each column, though you can do more if you like.

Words that contain the letter **T**	
2 T's Aim for 12	3 or more T's Aim for 1

Change and Rhyme 8

Change one letter in both words in the pair so they rhyme. For example, LIFT & WIRE becomes LIFE & WIFE.
There may be more than one solution.

SET & BLOG

SOUP & TONER

Q Crosswords 8

A straightforward crossword in the shape of a Q.

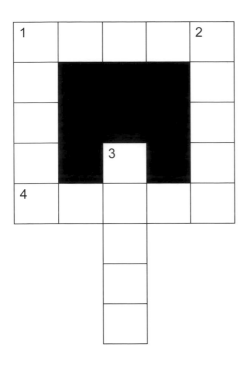

ACROSS
1. A greeting
4. A person, not an animal

DOWN
1. Rabbit's house
2. Regularly
3. Tiny

Wheel Words 8

Work out what the word in each wheel reads. The letters go in <u>either direction</u>, and the word can start anywhere in the wheel.
Topic: OCCUPATIONS

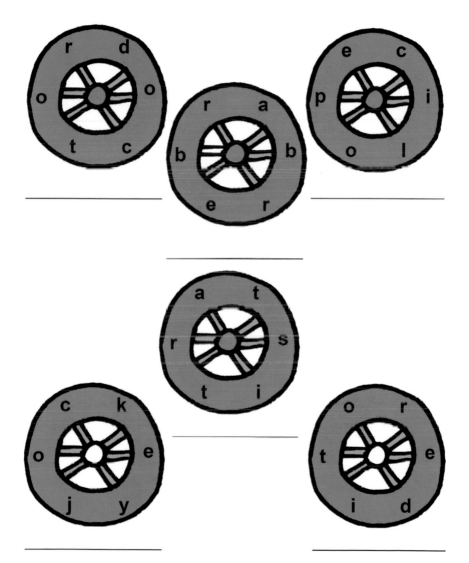

Weird & Wonderful Words 8

Make a new compound word by choosing a word from each column and joining them together.
Write a description of what this new word means, and then write a sentence showing how it's used.

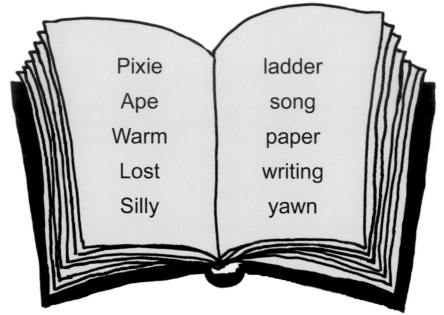

Pixie   ladder
Ape   song
Warm   paper
Lost   writing
Silly   yawn

WORD:

DESCRIPTION:

SENTENCE:

Remove a Letter 8

Take one letter out of each word so the words make a real sentence.
For example, if you take one letter out of each of these words, PIT HIS AN WHEN, it becomes IT IS A HEN.

THEY STARTS SHRINE

CAT KNIGHT

AEIOU 8

The vowels A E I O U are missing from the following words.
Work out which vowel goes in which word, but check carefully
before you write them in!
Cross off the vowels as you use them.

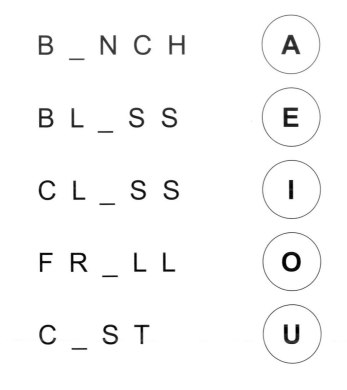

B _ N C H   **A**

B L _ S S   **E**

C L _ S S   **I**

F R _ L L   **O**

C _ S T   **U**

Skillful Sentences 8

Can you write a sentence—or sentences—where at least two words rhyme with the word "sleet"?

Level 9

Word Line 9

Start at the letter in the circle and draw a continuous line right, left, up, or down, and also <u>diagonally</u> to find the letters in the saying. The punctuation marks are not included.

"You have been my friend.
That in itself is a tremendous thing."
Charlotte's Web

t	s	e	l	f	a	t
i	n	i	h	i	s	r
n	i	g	t	o	d	e
h	a	t	s	u	n	m
t	d	n	n	e	e	e
i	e	m	o	u	b	e
r	f	y	(Y)	h	a	v

Umbrella Words 9

These umbrellas have letters on them. With the umbrella closed you can only see two letters. Work out words that might be written on the umbrella when it is open. The word has to contain these two letters in this order, but it can be as long or short as you like, and the letters can appear anywhere in the word. See if you can find different ways to include the letters in a word.

Train Words 9

Can you find the three-letter words hidden in the train cars?

all   ail   ill   air   aid   lid

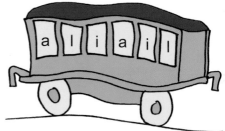

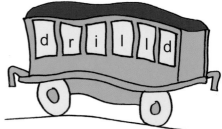

Anagrams 9

Work out the anagrams, then draw a line between the words that are word pairs.
Word pairs are two words that often go together; for example, "man and wife."

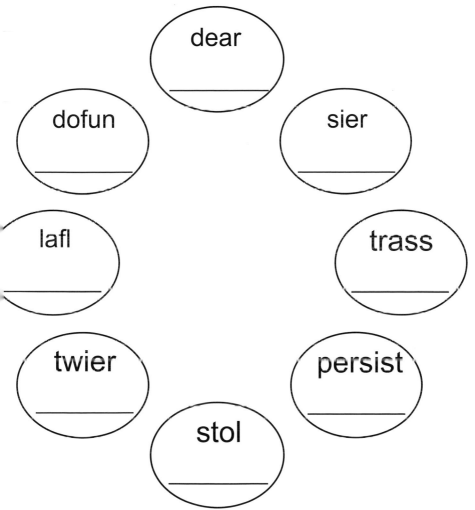

Alphabet Teasers 9

Choose words that fit into the grid using the letters given.

Begins with	Noun	Adjective	Verb
TH			
TR			
CH			
CR			

Fishing 9

Fish for the right letters to make words that solve the clues.

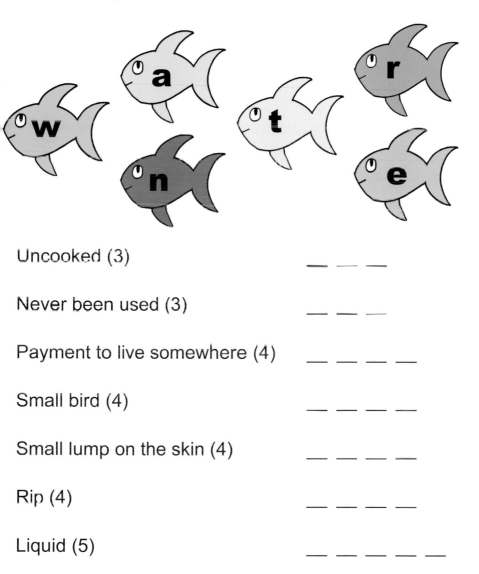

Uncooked (3)   __ __ __

Never been used (3)   __ __ __

Payment to live somewhere (4)   __ __ __ __

Small bird (4)   __ __ __ __

Small lump on the skin (4)   __ __ __ __

Rip (4)   __ __ __ __

Liquid (5)   __ __ __ __ __

Mini Word Sudoku 9

Place the letters from the six-letter word **"minute"** in the grid so that each column, each row, and each of the six 2×3 sub-grids contains all the six letters from the word.

	n	u			
				i	u
	t	n			
u			m		t
e		m	i		
				u	m

Alphabet 9

In the passage below, can you find words with two letters together that come next to each other in the alphabet? There are ten to find. The first one has been underlined for you.
Use the alphabet to help you: **a b c d e f g h i j k l m n o p q r s t u v w x y z**

"Calm down, you look like you've seen a

ghost," said Jordan's dad.

"I think I have—inside that open closet!"

replied Jordan.

"No, it wouldn't be able to get in. It's full of

tunics," smiled Dad.

Time to Rhyme 9

In each flower, put a circle around any words in the petals that rhyme with the word in the middle. Then write another word in the empty petal that rhymes with the word in the middle and ends in the underlined letters.

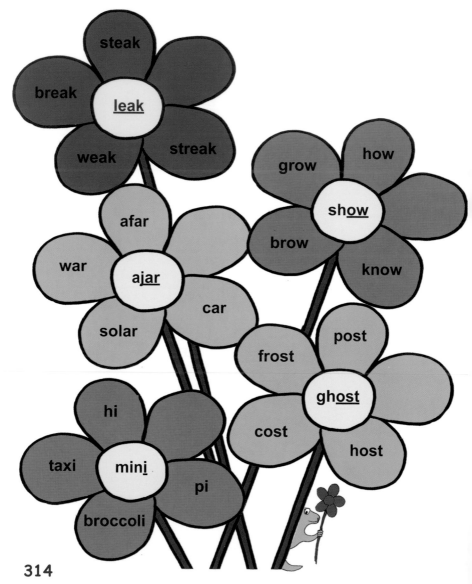

The Big X Word Search 9

The words to find are in pairs. You will find each pair of names in the shape of an X.

Can you find:
FLORA - ILONA
LIZZY - HAZEL
SALLY - MOLLY
JAYNE - KAYLA
ALICE - AKIRA

N	I	S	T	F	A	G	T	C	T	T	M
A	L	Ö	F	T	H	P	S	I	T	S	A
N	N	I	E	A	S	F	O	U	I	A	W
T	I	A	Z	G	F	F	A	L	S	W	L
T	E	E	S	Z	B	R	O	O	T	S	M
J	L	H	L	R	Y	T	Q	R	A	D	N
J	T	P	L	K	H	A	M	L	A	H	S
H	A	F	A	I	A	J	L	A	L	T	A
T	O	Y	D	J	J	L	K	D	W	Y	Y
A	L	M	N	I	C	B	I	L	A	N	I
A	M	N	T	E	M	R	C	H	L	G	S
H	L	G	A	H	A	A	C	B	E	L	G

The Word Store 9

The Word Store is a special place that sells different kinds of words. Today we are going shopping for **different types of words**. Wherever there is a space in the story, write in a word that starts with the letter given. It's a good idea to read through the story first to get a feel for what you may want to write. If you write in pencil, you can do the puzzle more than once and make the story different each time.

The Word Store

Rachel loved to make cupcakes. Everybody said they were

t _____, even

d _____.

She would make them every

w _____ and sell them at the

m _____. However, what people didn't

r _____ was that the cupcakes were made

from special ingredients—magical things like butterfly

t _____, a jar of r _____,

and a fairy's s _____.

She would s_____ them together with a

m _____ s _____ made from

enchanted silver.

Watching people eat her magical cupcakes made

Rachel very h_____.

Letters 9

Color the squares with **letters that have straight lines only** in **blue**. For example, the letter H.
Color the squares with **letters that have straight and curved lines** in brown. For example, the letter B.
Then work out what the picture is.

H	E	N	L	F	A
A	G	K	E	R	T
N	D	P	G	P	L
L	R	H	T	Q	A
M	P	R	P	G	H
A	Q	A	N	B	K
F	B	J	R	P	E
K	G	F	T	G	F
A	R	G	D	B	H
F	J	H	E	D	M
H	B	Q	J	R	E
E	J	F	M	P	K

Words and Sounds 9

Alliteration happens when words that start with the same sound are used in a row or near each other.

Write a sentence with at least four words that all start with the same sound. Note that sometimes the same letters may not have the same sound; for example, capital city.

The first one has been done for you.

P	Pauline patiently picks pretty pansies.
H	
L	
A	
B	
N	

Synonyms 9

A synonym is a word that means exactly or nearly the same as another word; for example, "sad" and "unhappy" are synonyms. Find the pairs of synonyms and draw a line connecting the two.

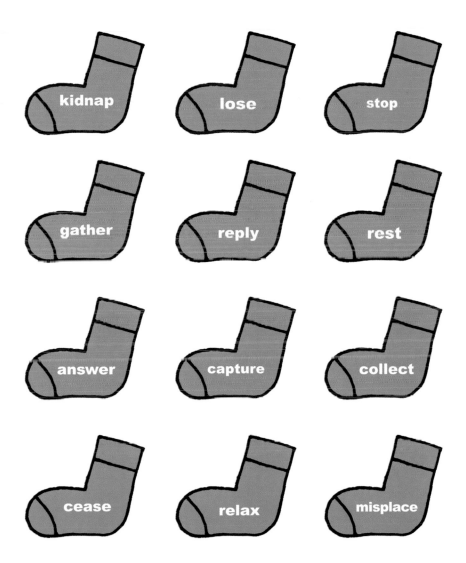

Acronyms 9

Acronyms are words formed from the initial letters of other words. For example, **ASPS** could stand for "American Society Protecting Snakes."

Work out what the three acronyms could stand for, then make up one of your own at the end.

Theme: ADVENTURE

Definitions 9

Choose the correct definition for each word.

Omega	1) Enormous 2) Last letter of the Greek alphabet 3) Object of good luck
Famished	1) Well-known 2) Extremely hungry 3) Popular
Summit	1) The top 2) Brief details 3) To call someone
Urban	1) Man's headdress 2) Smart 3) Living in a city
Heron	1) A warrior 2) Long-legged bird 3) A fish found in the Atlantic Ocean

Leaping Lizard 9

The words of a sentence have been jumbled up and placed onto rocks. The lizard is sitting by the rock with the first word. Work out which order the words go in, and draw a line to show the lizard which way to jump.
You can write the sentence at the bottom.

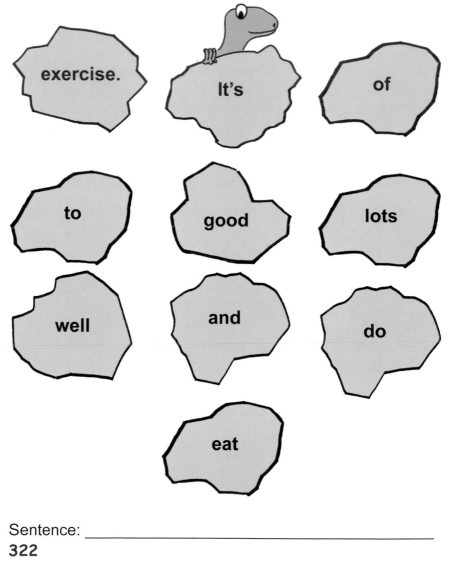

Sentence: _____

Syllables 9

Add a letter or letters to the ones already given to make words that are 1, 2, and 3 syllables long.

Note that the sound of the vowel may change; for example, "l<u>o</u>w" and "l<u>o</u>gic." That's okay.

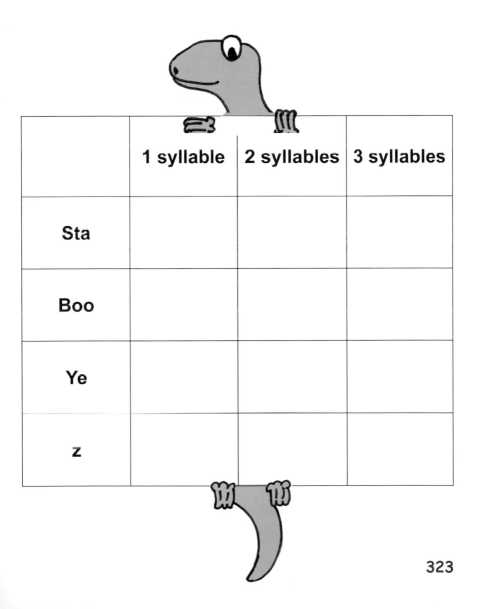

	1 syllable	2 syllables	3 syllables
Sta			
Boo			
Ye			
z			

Compound Words 9

A compound word is formed when two words join together to become a new word; for example, softball, teapot, and armchair.

Think of as many words as you can that could join onto the <u>beginning</u> of the given word to make a compound word.

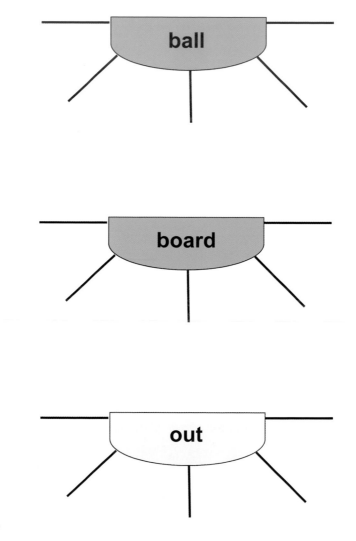

Continuous Words 9

This is a list of words joined together, with the word spaces taken out. How many can you find?
Topic: WORDS CONTAINING "W" AND "E"

sweetweststewweatherwhennewwenttowe
ltowerweeppowerwebbrewanswerweeddw
elllowerweektwelvetweetvoweltwentyflowe
rwerefew

Speed Words 9

Choose words that fit the description. Use words that don't start with a capital letter, and use a different word for each question.

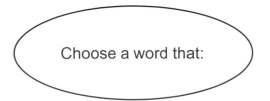

Choose a word that:

1	Contains "ING" but not at the end of the word	
2	Starts and ends with K	
3	Has the structure: consonant vowel consonant consonant	
4	Is an anagram of RONGAD	
5	Ends in "GY"	

Concentration 9

Read the passage and answer the questions at the end.

Flying with a Dragon

Rex flew around the volcano breathing huge flames and roaring "RAARGH!" while the scared villagers ran for cover.

"Grrr," growled Wilfred. "Uurgh," mumbled Wilma.

Rex tried not to laugh. Next, he swooped menacingly over the muddy swamps.

"RAARGH!" he roared as people jumped into the mud to hide.

"Grrr," growled Wilfred. "Uurgh," mumbled Wilma.

Rex tried *very hard* not to laugh. Finally, he flew over the dark, sinister forest and set the tops of the trees on fire. **"RAARGH!"**

QUESTIONS

1. How many words start with the letter R? _____

2. How many verbs are in the past tense? _____

Vocabulary 9

Fit the three-letter words into the correct spaces in the larger words.

LAY ATE RIG ELL APT HIS RID

A L __ __ __ H T

W __ __ __ P E R

C __ __ __ U R E

P __ __ __ E R

H E __ __ __ R

A S T __ __ __ E

S M __ __ __ Y

Change a Letter 9

Change one letter in the word, so that it fits the definition.

Word	Definition	New word
LIME	Arm or leg	
WARY	Pleasant temperature	
BURN	Put or hide underground	
FURL	Containing as much as possible	
CASE	Money	
TOIL	Implement	
WHEN	Small bird	
SOAP	Sudden bite	
OARS	Fights or conflicts	
WHIT	Stay until something happens	

Hat Words 9

Fill in the rows with words that include the letter T. Try not to use plurals.

Categories 9

The list contains words that fall into two categories: American spelling and British spelling.
Write the words into the correct category in the balloon.

center   tyres   labour   realize   pajamas   programme

centre   tires   labor   realise   pyjamas   program

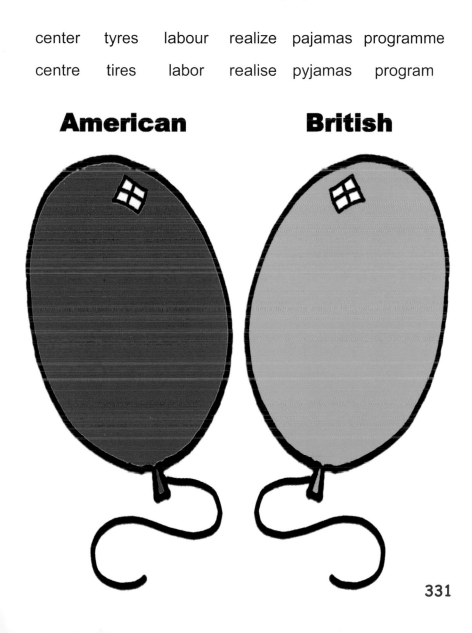

American

British

Gridword 9

Place the words so they fit in the grid. A letter has been filled in for you.

STREET

SPONGE

ASCENT

CLOSET

SLEEPS

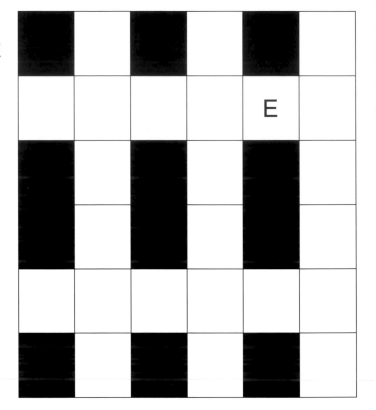

Lizard in a Cave 9

Each cave has an anagram of food or drink.
Today the lizard wants to go in the cave with **something to drink**. Solve the anagrams and write the words beneath the caves, then color in or put a circle around the cave the lizard would like to go in.

How Many 9

How many words can you think of that contain the letter **P**? There can be any other vowels and consonants in the word, and the letter P can come anywhere.

Aim for the number stated in each column, though you can do more if you like.

Words that contain the letter **P**	
2 P's Aim for 10	3 or more P's Aim for 2

Change and Rhyme 9

Change one letter in both words in the pair so they rhyme. For example, LIFT & WIRE becomes LIFE & WIFE.
There may be more than one solution.

SIGH & MICE

ANY & PANE

Q Crosswords 9

A straightforward crossword in the shape of a Q.

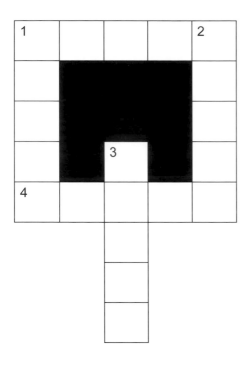

ACROSS

1. It could be a horn-less unicorn!
4. Food in the middle of the day

DOWN

1. You can book a room here
2. Our planet
3. Not over

Wheel Words 9

Work out what the word in each wheel reads. The letters go in <u>either direction</u>, and the word can start anywhere in the wheel.
Topic: ADEJCTIVES

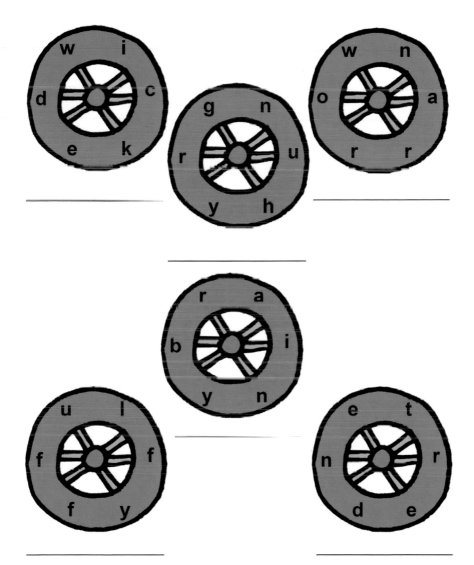

1. WICKED
2. HUNGRY
3. NARROW
4. BRAINY
5. FLUFFY
6. TENDER

Weird & Wonderful Words 9

Make a new compound word by choosing a word from each column and joining them together.
Write a description of what this new word means, and then write a sentence showing how it's used.

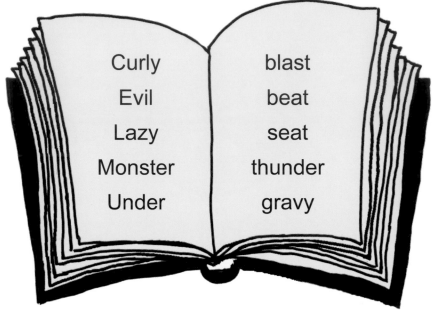

Curly   blast

Evil   beat

Lazy   seat

Monster   thunder

Under   gravy

WORD:

DESCRIPTION:

SENTENCE:

Remove a Letter 9

Take one letter out of each word so the words make a real sentence.
For example, if you take one letter out of each of these words, PIT HIS AN WHEN, it becomes IT IS A HEN.

HEN BROUGHT OPEN

LAND PAMPER

A E I O U 9

The vowels A E I O U are missing from the following words. Work out which vowel goes in which word, but check carefully before you write them in!
Cross off the vowels as you use them.

G L _ V E   **A**

S T _ P   **E**

C L _ B   **I**

G R _ B   **O**

S P O _ L   **U**

Skillful Sentences 9

Can you write a sentence—or sentences—with at least four words, where each word contains a double letter?

Level 10

Word Line 10

Start at the letter in the circle and draw a continuous line right, left, up or down, and also <u>diagonally</u> to find the letters in the saying. The punctuation marks are not included.

"If you have good thoughts, they will shine out of your face like sunbeams."

Roald Dahl

u	t	c	e	e	s	u
o	o	l	a	k	a	n
e	f	f	i	m	e	b
n	y	r	s	(l)	f	y
i	o	u			h	u	o
h	s				a	v
l	l	s	t	h	g	e
w	i	t	h	o	u	g
y	e	h	t	d	o	o

Umbrella Words 10

These umbrellas have letters on them. With the umbrella closed you can only see two letters. Work out words that might be written on the umbrella when it is open. The word has to contain these two letters in this order, but it can be as long or short as you like, and the letters can appear anywhere in the word. See if you can find different ways to include the letters in a word.

j e

p u

d w

e o

Train Words 10

Can you find the three-letter words hidden in the train cars?

see   tee   bee   set   bet   ebb

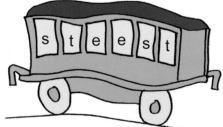

Anagrams 10

Work out the anagrams, then draw a line between the words that are word pairs.
Word pairs are two words that often go together; for example, "man and wife."

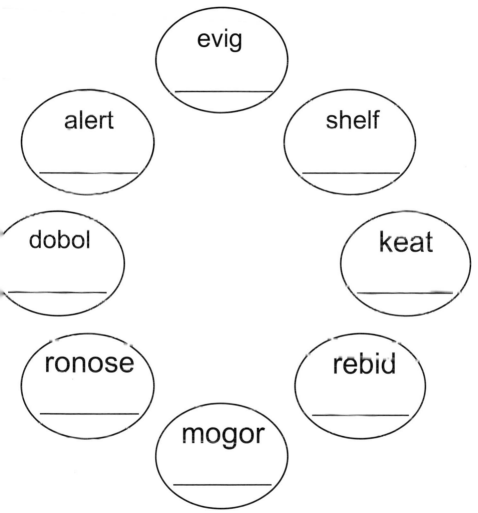

Alphabet Teasers 10

Choose words that fit into the grid using the letters given. Use a different word for each part of the grid.

Begins with	Noun	Adjective	Verb
SW			
FR			
PL			
QU			

Fishing 10

Fish for the right letters to make words that solve the clues.

Request (3)

___ ___ ___

Money (4)

___ ___ ___ ___

Large bag (4)

___ ___ ___ ___

Hut (5)

___ ___ ___ ___ ___

Soft, light-colored rock (5)

___ ___ ___ ___ ___

Not tight; loose (5)

___ ___ ___ ___ ___

Fight (5)

___ ___ ___ ___ ___

Mini Word Sudoku 10

Place the letters from the six-letter word **"action"** in the grid so that each column, each row, and each of the six 2×3 sub-grids contains all the six letters from the word.

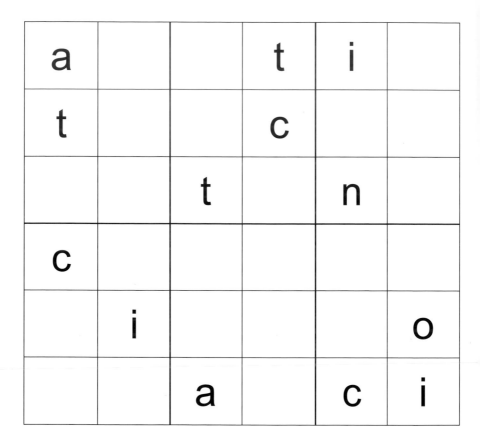

Time to Rhyme 10

In each flower, put a circle around any words in the petals that rhyme with the word in the middle. Then write another word in the empty petal that rhymes with the word in the middle and ends in the underlined letters.

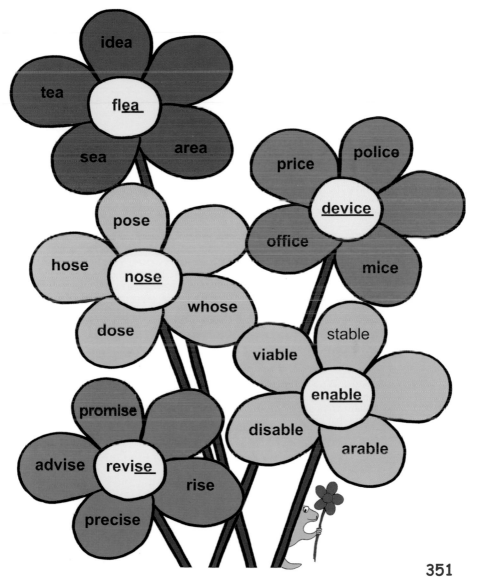

Alphabet 10

In the passage below, can you find words with two letters together that come next to each other in the alphabet? There are ten to find.

Use the alphabet to help you: **a b c d e f g h i j k l m n o p q r s t u v w x y z**

"Quickly—go left, and we'll make it to the Roxy cinema in time."

"What's this movie about?"

"Omnivore tigers."

"Seriously, dude?"

"Well, not just that . . ."

The Big X Word Search 10

The words to find are in pairs. You will find each pair of countries in the shape of an X.

Can you find:
CHILE - CHINA
CONGO - KENYA
JAPAN - NEPAL
GHANA - ITALY
WALES - MALTA

K	U	B	R	A	G	T	I	I	E	A	A
E	C	I	S	W	C	H	T	S	P	H	F
T	N	H	G	II	I	S	L	B	N	S	A
D	G	I	I	S	I	L	N	P	Y	R	H
C	S	N	L	L	Y	M	C	A	S	C	K
C	A	G	M	A	E	E	E	I	O	G	C
C	D	R	C	C	E	E	G	N	R	T	S
W	Z	S	A	M	N	C	C	J	Y	B	V
B	A	G	A	F	G	E	A	P	U	A	O
C	F	L	I	C	I	I	S	H	K	C	P
J	T	T	E	P	A	A	A	Z	Q	I	N
A	S	A	U	S	N	A	E	B	L	C	H

The Word Store 10

The Word Store is a special place that sells different kinds of words. Today we are going shopping for **different types of words**. Wherever there is a space in the story, write in a word that starts with the letter given. It's a good idea to read through the story first to get a feel for what you may want to write. If you write in pencil, you can do the puzzle more than once and make the story different each time.

The Word Store

Every time Tom walked past the gallery he saw some

b _____

p _____ in there.

He didn't b _____

any, but he did a _____ them.

One day there was a t _____ storm that

d _____ everything in the town. Everything, that is, except the things in the gallery that Tom walked past.

"How o _____," he thought. "Have some

s _____ forces been at play?"

He decided to i _____.

All kinds of things were in there; unusual things like

b _____ made from f _____ and

c_____ made from l_____.

354

Letters 10

Color the squares with **letters that have straight lines** only (for example, the letter H) in **blue**.

Color the squares with **curved lines only** (for example, the letter S) in **red**.

Color the squares with **letters that have straight and curved lines** (for example, the letter B) in **gray**.

Then work out what the picture is.

F	T	I	H	Y	F	K	N	M	L	E	H
B	A	Q	R	G	A	M	W	V	Z	A	H
G	R	P	N	V	I	F	K	T	A	D	J
R	J	B	F	D	H	P	E	G	W	Q	G
B	J	Q	D	Q	R	P	B	R	Q	B	D
G	G	P	B	J	C	S	G	D	Q	O	C
Q	D	G	P	R	C	O	J	P	B	C	S
H	O	S	Q	R	G	D	S	O	R	R	D

355

Words and Sounds 10

Alliteration happens when words that start with the same sound are used in a row or near each other.
Write a sentence with at least four words that all start with the same sound. Note that sometimes the same letters may not have the same sound; for example, <u>c</u>apital <u>c</u>ity.

T	
C	
S	
E	
PH	

Synonyms 10

A synonym is a word that means exactly or nearly the same as another word; for example, "sad" and "unhappy" are synonyms. Find the pairs of synonyms and draw a line connecting the two.

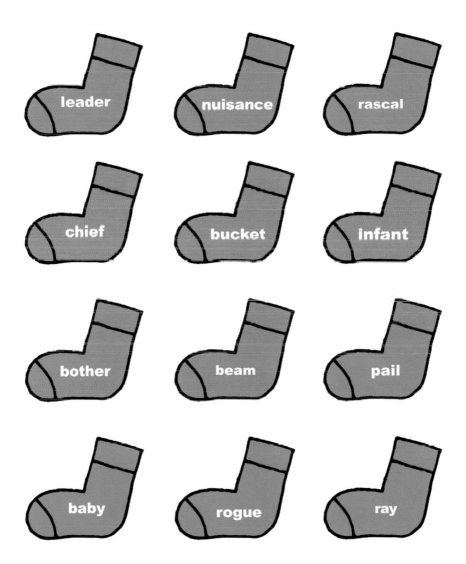

Acronyms 10

Acronyms are words formed from the initial letters of other words. For example, **ASPS** could stand for "American Society Protecting Snakes."

Work out what the three acronyms could stand for, then make up one of your own at the end.

Theme: COMMUNITY GROUPS

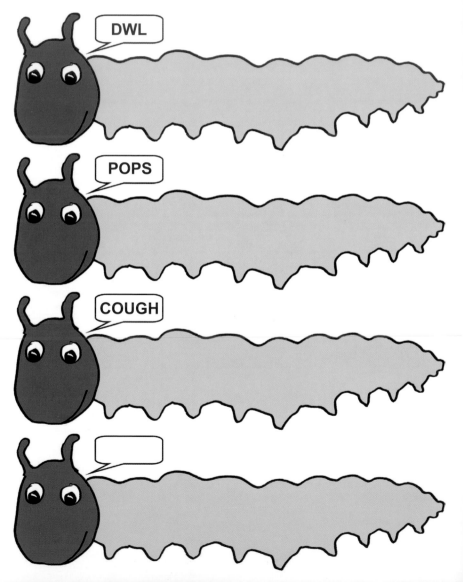

Definitions 10

Choose the correct definition for each word.

Typhoon	1) A powerful person 2) An illness 3) A hurricane
Phobia	1) A strong fear 2) A small watch on a chain 3) A moon that orbits a planet
Tigon	1) The prong of a fork 2) A creature born from a tiger and lioness 3) A stringed instrument
Thistle	1) A prickly plant 2) A shrill sound 3) To carve
Naïve	1) A dishonest man 2) Water nymph 3) Innocent

Leaping Lizard 10

The words of a sentence have been jumbled up and placed onto rocks. The lizard is sitting by the rock with the first word. Work out which order the words go in, and draw a line to show the lizard which way to jump.

You can write the sentence at the bottom.

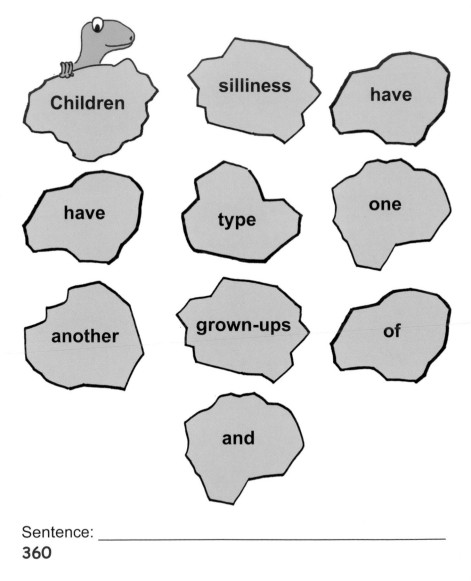

Sentence: _____

Syllables 10

Add a letter or letters to the ones already given to make words that are 1, 2, and 3 syllables long.
Note that the sound of the vowel may change; for example, "l<u>o</u>w" and "l<u>o</u>gic." That's okay.

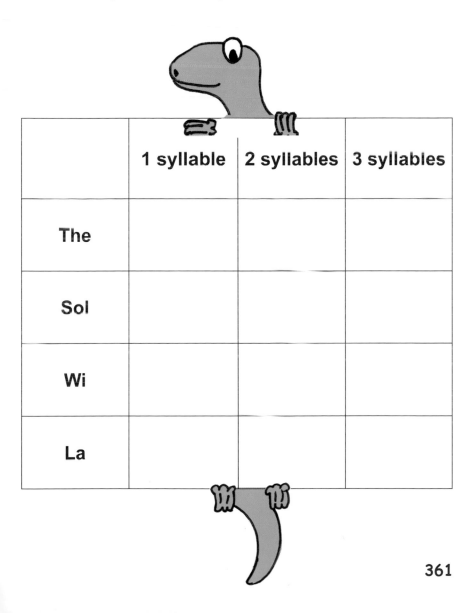

	1 syllable	2 syllables	3 syllables
The			
Sol			
Wi			
La			

Compound Words 10

A compound word is formed when two words join together to become a new word; for example, softball, teapot, and armchair.

Can you work out what the compound words are from their definition? The first letter is given.

F	Two weeks
B	Insect with large, brightly colored wings
E	Small burrowing creature that lives in the soil
B	A large hall for dancing
S	Sit or lie outside to tan the skin
S	Sea animal with five arms
H	Flat, round mixture of meat served in a bread roll
H	A holiday for a newly married couple
P	Official document used to travel abroad

Continuous Words 10

This is a list of words joined together with the word spaces taken out. How many can you find?
Topic: WORDS CONTAINING "B" AND "L"

belowblessbluebubblebellnobleblooddabb
leblendbelttremblebladeblandhumbleblam
ebaldablebelongoblongblogblowbowlblan
kbalancebleachrumblebull

Speed Words 10

Choose words that fit the description. Use words that don't start with a capital letter, and use a different word for each question.

Choose a word that:

1	Has the structure: vowel consonant vowel consonant vowel	
2	Starts with V and has 6 letters	
3	Fits into M __ M __ __ __	
4	Starts with I and ends in O	
5	Has 6 letters but only 1 syllable	

Concentration 10

Read the passage and answer the questions at the end.

Back Home

The week had ended, the potion had worn off, and Wilma and Wilfred went back home where they were a witch and wizard again.

"Where were you?" asked Wilfred's neighbor.

"The witch and I were having an adventure where the dragon lives."

"Which witch were you with?"

"Wilma the witch who lives where the wood starts."

"Where which wood starts?"

"The wood where you and I were looking for a witch to borrow a broomstick from."

"Where were you planning to go next with the witch?"

"Where the witch's broomstick wants to go."

QUESTIONS

How many of each of these words can you find:

Which _____ Witch _____ Where _____ Were _____

Vocabulary 10

Fit the three-letter words into the correct spaces in the larger words.

OFF   LOB   LEA   LOT   POO   EAT   LIE   UGH

_ _ _ R L Y

C _ _ _ E E

P _ _ _ S U R E

C _ _ _ H E S

B E _ _ _ V E

T H O _ _ _ T

B E N _ _ _ H

G _ _ _ E

Change a Letter 10

Change one letter in the word so it fits the definition.

Word	Definition	New word
ACNE	Measurement of land area	
EARN	Farm building	
ARUM	Musical instrument	
WILY	Slippery, greasy	
AUNT	Chase	
SINK	Animal noise	
AWAY	Lean unsteadily	
STEM	Article, thing	
DOZE	Leak out	
KNIT	Individual thing	

Hat Words 10

Fill in the rows with words that include the letter X. Try not to use plurals.

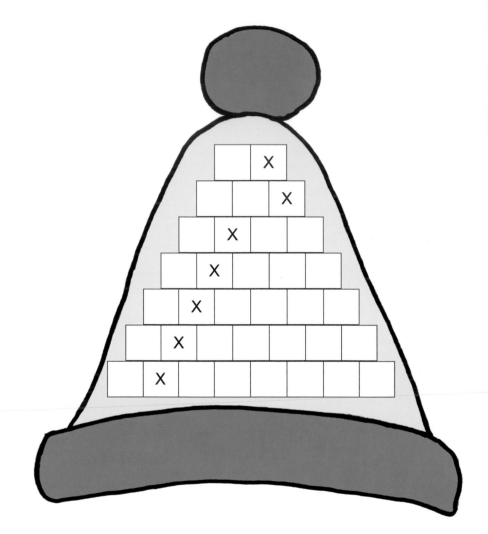

Categories 10

The list contains words that fall into three categories: words that come from the Japanese language, words that come from the Italian language, and words that come from the French language. Write the words into the correct category in the balloons.

sushi   pizza   judo   table   lasagna   grand

risotto   voyage   pardon   pasta   karaoke   sumo

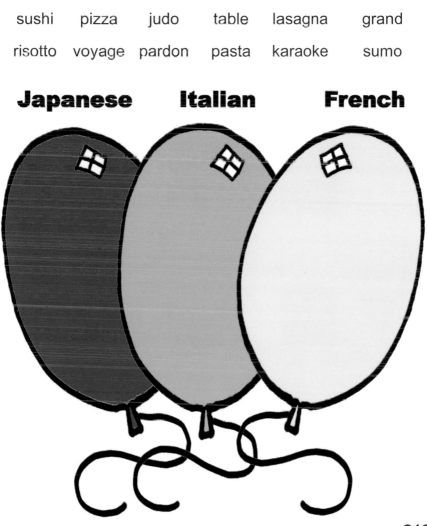

Japanese   **Italian**   **French**

Gridword 10

Place the words so they fit in the grid. A letter has been filled in for you.

STATUE

TATTOO

COFFEE

STOATS

KARATE

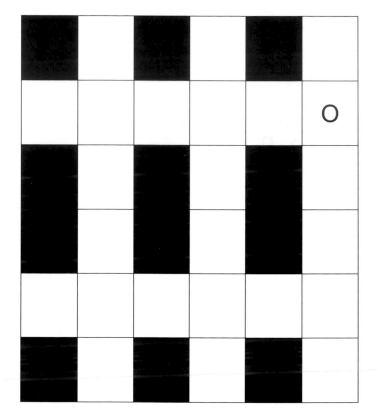

Lizard in a Cave 10

Each cave has an anagram of a creature.
Today the lizard wants to go in the cave with another **reptile**.
Solve the anagrams and write the words beneath the caves,
then color in or put a circle around the cave the lizard would
like to go in.

How Many 10

How many words can you think of that contain the letter **B**? There can be any other vowels and consonants in the word, and the letter B can come anywhere.

Aim for the number stated in each column, though you can do more if you like.

Words that contain the letter **B**	
2 B's Aim for 10	3 or more B's Aim for 2

Change and Rhyme 10

Change one letter in both words in the pair so that they rhyme.
For example, LIFT & WIRE becomes LIFE & WIFE.
There may be more than one solution.

MAID & BET

PLAN & THEN

Q Crosswords 10

A straightforward crossword in the shape of a Q.

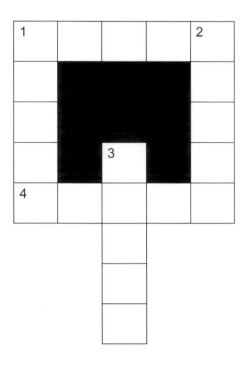

ACROSS
1. A cheap fruit? (anagram)
4. In a rage

DOWN
1. Round, flat Italian food
2. Pleased
3. A spy is a secret one of these

Wheel Words 10

Work out what the word in each wheel reads. The letters go in <u>either direction</u>, and the word can start anywhere in the wheel.
Topic: FOOD

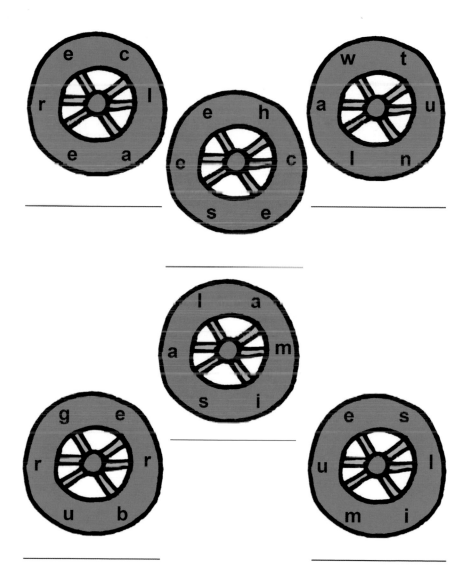

Weird & Wonderful Words 10

Make a new compound word by choosing a word from each column and joining them together.
Write a description of what this new word means, and then write a sentence showing how it's used.

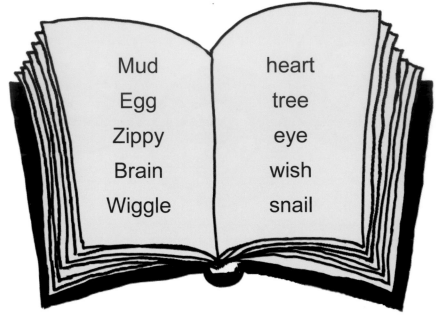

Mud	heart
Egg	tree
Zippy	eye
Brain	wish
Wiggle	snail

WORD:

DESCRIPTION:

SENTENCE:

Remove a Letter 10

Take one letter out of each word so the words make a real sentence.
For example, if you take one letter out of each of these words, PIT HIS AN WHEN, it becomes IT IS A HEN.

HI SOFTEN TREAD

MANDY BROOKS

A E I O U 10

The vowels A E I O U are missing from the following words. Work out which vowel goes in which word, but check carefully before you write them in!
Cross off the vowels as you use them.

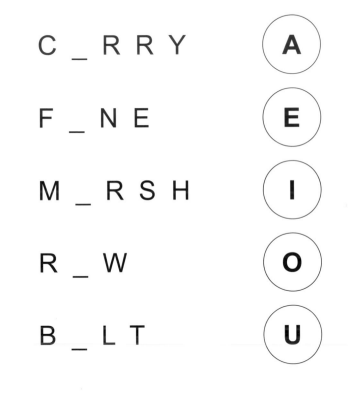

C _ R R Y   **A**

F _ N E   **E**

M _ R S H   **I**

R _ W   **O**

B _ L T   **U**

Skillful Sentences 10

Can you write a sentence—or sentences—with at least four words where all the words are made from letters in the first half of the alphabet? You can use the letters as often as you like. The letters are: A B C D E F G H I J K L M

Bonus Puzzles

Adjectives and Nouns 1

Think of an adjective and noun that both start and end with the same letter. For example, **E**normou**S** **E**ar**S**.
For the first three, the adjectives are given, while for the second three, you can think up both the adjective and the noun.

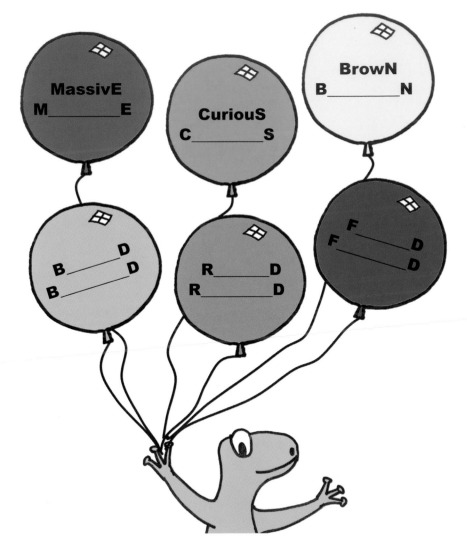

Vowel Swap 1

The vowels in these words have been swapped. Work out the correct version, then write them into the story below. The first one has been done for you.

Word with the vowels swapped	Word with the vowels in the right order
BLENKAT	BLANKET
CERPAT	
METHOR	
PECKID	
POLLIW	
SAFO	
TEBLA	
TEMI	

"It's _____ for bed," said my _____, so I got off the _____ , _____ my books off the _____, and put them on the _____. After going to the bathroom, I snuggled under the <u>BLANKET</u>, my head on the soft _____.

Number Words 1

Choose words that fit the description. Use words that don't start with a capital letter, and use different words for each question.

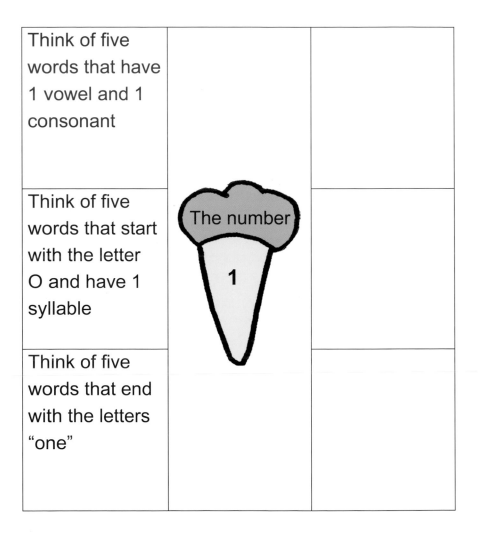

Think of five words that have 1 vowel and 1 consonant		
Think of five words that start with the letter O and have 1 syllable		
Think of five words that end with the letters "one"		

Answers

WORD LINE 1

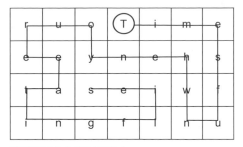

UMBRELLA WORDS 1
There are many suitable answers, for example:
fl: flag, flower, trifle
te: tea, tent, gate
or: orange, over, corn

TRAIN WORDS 1
The words to find have been underlined:
com<u>bat</u>, ka<u>yak</u>, <u>tram</u>ps, es<u>cape</u>, <u>scat</u>ty, <u>grat</u>ed

ANAGRAMS 1
cold hot; big small; near far; down up

ALPHABET TEASERS 1
There are many suitable answers, for example

Begins with	Animal	Place	Boy's name
T	Tiger	Texas	Tom
S	Snake	Spain	Samuel
P	Panda	Paris	Paul
L	Lizard	London	Liam

FISHING 1
net, one, ten, nose, rose, snore, stone

MINI WORD SUDOKU 1

r	d	e	a
e	a	d	r
d	r	a	e
a	e	r	d

ALPHABET 1
open, shut

TIME TO RHYME 1
There are several suitable answers, including:
CAT: bat, hat, mat, pat, sat
GOAT: boat, coat, moat, note, wrote

PIG: big, dig, fig, jig, rig
SHEEP: deep, jeep, heap, leap, peep
LAMB: clam, ham, jam, pram, tram

THE BIG X WORD SEARCH 1

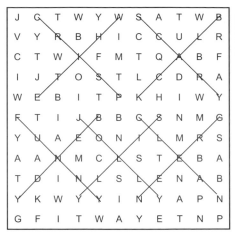

THE WORD STORE 1
There could be many answers, including:
Alice was an active girl who had a very bossy brother called Callum. Alice wanted a cute cat, but Callum preferred a dangerous dog, and they couldn't agree. "Why don't we get an elegant bird?" asked Mom. "Or a fluffy rabbit instead?" "No," said Callum. "Birds are gross!" "But a happy rabbit would be okay," said Alice. "Perhaps we could get it an interesting hutch to live in." "Okay," said Callum "as long as it's a jumping rabbit." "Great," said Mom. "We'll go to the pet shop tomorrow."

LETTERS 1

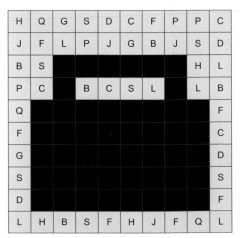

WORDS AND SOUNDS 1

Every ~~weak~~ / week Joy goes for / ~~four~~ a walk in the park. She likes ~~too~~ / to look at the colorful ~~flours~~ / flowers along the path. Her favorite is a red rose / ~~rows~~. "It's beautiful," she ~~side~~ / sighed. "Especially when the sun / ~~son~~ shines on it." "Hi!" / ~~High!~~ called out her friend Rachel. "It's good to ~~sea~~ / see you. Shall we go for a walk along the ~~beech~~ / beach later?"

SYNONYMS 1

House home, money cash, road street, question query, steam mist, type sort

ACRONYMS 1

There are many suitable answers, for example:
SoLL Society of Lizard Lovers
PADO Puppy and Dog Organization

DEFINITIONS 1

Imaginary 3) Not real
Albino 2) Person with white skin and hair, and pink eyes
Asterisk 3) A star-shaped symbol
Narrator 1) Person who tells a story
Floppy 2) Soft and bendy

LEAPING LIZARD 1

You can never have too many books.

SYLLABLES 1

There are many suitable answers, for example:
Cart Carpet Carpenter
Bank Banjo Banana
Men Messy Medicine

COMPOUND WORDS 1

Handshake, lifeguard, grandson, moonbeam, anywhere, keyhole, horseshoe, headboard, earring

CONTINUOUS WORDS 1

Corn asparagus spinach cucumber radish broccoli cauliflower turnip peas cabbage celery lettuce beetroot tomato potato onion carrot pumpkin bean pepper sprouts

SPEED WORDS 1

There are many suitable answers, for example:
1. YEAR, 2. TWEET, 3. HOOP, 4. SILLY, 5. VERY

CONCENTRATION 1

The nouns have been underlined:
Wilma gets it wrong. Wilma is a kind and mischievous witch who lives in the woods. She has a broomstick and a black cat and likes to play tricks on people. One Saturday she felt bored and decided to fly into the next wood where she saw a family eating a picnic. "I see a young boy being naughty," she said to herself. "I will turn him into a big brown toad to teach him a lesson!" However, the young boy liked being a toad. He jumped onto the sandwiches and into the bowl of cream and then ate the strawberries. "Hmm," thought Wilma, "this hasn't worked. I will have to change him back."

VOCABULARY 1

PIMPLE PANDA PEBBLE PILLOW PANTHER PARTNER

CHANGE A LETTER 1

BEAR, DEAR, FEAR, WINE, PINK, PANE, REST, PAST, NEST

HAT WORDS 1

There are many suitable answers, for example:
A, TO, CAR, LIME, KNIFE, HELPER, TEENAGE, TREASURE

CATEGORIES 1

COLORS: BEIGE, CRIMSON, INDIGO, BRONZE, JADE, RUSSET
TASTES: BITTER, ACIDIC, SALTY, MILD, SPICY, SOUR

GRIDWORD 1

H	O	N	E	Y
O		E		O
T	I	R	E	D
E		V		E
L	O	Y	A	L

LIZARD IN A CAVE 1

The cave he would like to go in is underlined.
HORSE SNAKE TIGER SHEEP MOOSE

HOW MANY 1

There are many suitable answers, for example:
1: CAT, ART, CART, HAM, LAMB, LAP, LAY, PAN, PAY, TAP
2: ALARM, AWAY
3: BANANA

CHANGE AND RHYME 1

There may be more than one solution
NEST & REST, BEE & KNEE

Q CROSSWORDS 1

ACROSS. 1. MOUSE, 4. YACHT
DOWN. 1. MUMMY, 2. EIGHT, 3. ACTOR

WHEEL WORDS 1

RABBIT, MONKEY, JAGUAR, LIZARD, BADGER

REMOVE A LETTER 1

THE CAT SAT ON THE MAT

AEIOU 1

PITY, WEST, HOLD, WAKE, CRUSH

SKILLFUL SENTENCES 1

There are many suitable answers, for example:
She saw six smiling students studying science.

IN THE MIDDLE 1
March April May, Beginning Middle End, Egg Chicken Hen, Cold Warm Hot, Two Four Six, Good Better Best, Black Gray White, Bronze Silver Gold.

WORD LINE 2

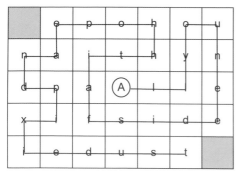

UMBRELLA WORDS 2
There are many suitable answers, for example:
gr: grin girl hungry
sh: shed such dash
ee: green ever fence
ba: bake boat cobra

TRAIN WORDS 2
The words to find have been underlined:
preyed, pearly, tribal, tulips, allege, warmer

ANAGRAMS 2
New old; short long; high low; bad good

ALPHABET TEASERS 2
There are many suitable answers, for example:

Begins with	Food	Color	Girl's name
G	Grape	Green	Grace
R	Rice	Red	Rose
B	Bread	Blue	Barbara
P	Pizza	Pink	Pauline

FISHING 2
Hat, ear, sea, seat, hear, heart, stare

MINI WORD SUDOKU 2

r	o	d	w
w	d	o	r
d	w	r	o
o	r	w	d

ALPHABET 2
Name of color: blue

TIME TO RHYME 2
There are several suitable answers, including:
THREE: bee, free, he, knee, tea
FOUR: core, door, pour, score, your
FIVE: dive, drive, hive, jive, live
SIX: bricks, fix, mix, picks, sticks
EIGHT: crate, date, mate, rate, state

THE BIG X WORD SEARCH 2

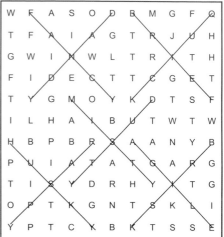

THE WORD STORE 2
There could be many answers, including: Norman was very naughty and sometimes his mom wished he was ordinary. His sister Pauline was very pleasant and usually quiet. One day Norman was being more rude than ever and his mom shouted, "Stop being silly! I'm too tired to cope with it." Norman looked upset so his dad said, "We all need to do something wild! Let's go for a drive, buy some yummy ice cream, and then go to the beach."

LETTERS 2

d	j	c	s	y	v	c	r	d	g
v	b	p	f	g	b	y	h	p	r
h				r	f				j
c				s	g				h
b				j	y				v
s	d	y	f	r	d	g	f	b	s
v	p	c	h	v	h	s	d	c	g
j	c							p	r
s	b							b	
c	r	v	g	p	y	j	h	d	p

WORDS AND SOUNDS 2

Behind ~~sum~~ / some bushes was a haunted house. "We're / ~~were~~ not ~~aloud~~ / allowed to go ~~their~~ / there," said Kira. "~~Your~~ / You're right," replied Mark. "It's too scary by / ~~bye~~ far." "A ghostly knight / ~~night~~ wearing ~~steal~~ / steel armor and riding a white horse, / ~~hoarse~~ can be ~~scene~~ / seen on Halloween."

SYNONYMS 2

Evil wicked, tiny little, large big, fast quick, kind helpful, lucky fortunate

ACRONYMS 2

There are many suitable answers, for example:
CLO Crossword Lovers' Organization
SIS Sudoku in Seattle
PSS Puzzle Solvers' Society

DEFINITIONS 2

Yak 1) An ox
Mischief 2) Naughtiness
Pomegranate 1) Tropical fruit
Truffle 3) A fungus you can eat
Fierce 2) Violent, angry

LEAPING LIZARD 2

A hug a day keeps the sadness away.

SYLLABLES 2

There are many suitable answers, for example:
Mark Market Marathon
Leg Lesson Lemonade
Fan Faster Favorite
Cone Connect Conference

COMPOUND WORDS 2

Eggcup, passport, walkway, eyebrow, cupboard, bagpipes, handbag, boardwalk, somewhere

CONTINUOUS WORDS 2

Cricket termite centipede bee beetle spider snail ladybug grub butterfly grasshopper flea ant maggot mosquito moth caterpillar dragonfly cockroach wasp locust cicada

SPEED WORDS 2

There are many suitable answers, for example:
1. LEAF, 2. ALIVE, 3. GREAT or GRATE, 4. TEACHER, 5. CORNER

CONCENTRATION 2

The adjectives have been underlined:
Wilma wonders what to do. Wilma was puzzled. "What can I do to give that naughty boy a lesson?" she wondered. "Cody!" she heard the boy's weary mother call. "If you don't stop being snotty I'll make you walk to the river and carry back a heavy bucket of water." "You can't make me," rude Cody replied. "Take the big blue bucket," his mom said, "and bring back plenty of fresh water." "No!" Cody answered back, sitting down on the upturned blue bucket.

VOCABULARY 2

SENDER SALESMAN SEARCH SOUTHERN SELFISH SOLIDER

CHANGE A LETTER 2

WIRE, TORE, TIDE, SEW, SAD, JAW, BORN, COIN, CORE

HAT WORDS 2

There are many suitable answers, for example:
A, AN, AND, ABLE, ALIVE, ARTIST, ANOTHER, ALTHOUGH

CATEGORIES 2

FRUIT: APPLE, PEAR, BANANA, PEACH, LIME, TANGERINE
VEGETABLE: CORN, CELERY, CARROT, CABBAGE, PEA, PUMPKIN

GRIDWORD 2

P	L	U	M	P
L		N		O
E	L	D	E	R
A		E		E
D	A	R	E	D

LIZARD IN A CAVE 2

The cave he would like to go in is underlined:
CLOUD WATER <u>GRASS</u> RIVER BEACH

HOW MANY 2

There are many suitable answers, for example:
1: BED, BET, EGG, LET, MEN, NEST, PET, RED, SHED, WEST
2: BEEF, DEER, FREE, HERE, NEED, SHEEP
3. CHEESE, DELETE

CHANGE AND RHYME 2

There may be more than one solution
SQUASH & POSH, BEAT & HEAT

Q CROSSWORDS 2

ACROSS. 1. CAROL, 4. SPOON
DOWN. 1. CHESS, 2. LEMON, 3. POPPY

WHEEL WORDS 2

CHERRY, TOMATO, BANANA, POTATO, RADISH

REMOVE A LETTER 2

THE BOY SAW HIS AUNT

AEIOU 2

PLUM, COLD, SOAP, MEN, SUIT

SKILLFUL SENTENCES 2

There are many suitable answers, for example:
Mark will walk home with Anne. Next week they will bike over here.

IN THE MIDDLE 2

Romeo and Juliet, Knife Fork Spoon, Three Little Pigs, Mercury Venus Earth, Baby Child Adult, How are you?, Stars and Stripes, Henry the Eighth.

WORD LINE 3

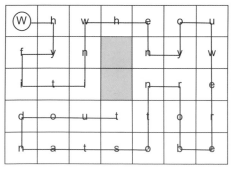

UMBRELLA WORDS 3

There are many suitable answers, for example:
oo: food motor oblong
dr: drop dear under
at: hat atlas past
li: like slip tulip

TRAIN WORDS 3

The words to find have been underlined: stints, octopi, apathy, spotty, ignite, staple

ANAGRAMS 3

easy hard; fast slow; happy sad; strong weak

ALPHABET TEASERS 3

There are many suitable answers, for example:

Begins with	Country	Flower, plant or tree	Bird
C	Chile	Cactus	Cuckoo
S	Spain	Snowdrop	Swallow
F	France	Fern	Finch
M	Mexico	Maple	Magpie

FISHING 3

Hoe, she, hole, sole, shoe, shell, hello

MINI WORD SUDOKU 3

i	e	**a**	d
a	d	**e**	i
d	**a**	i	**e**
e	**i**	d	a

ALPHABET 3

Elephant, elk, horse, hound, jackal, jaguar, moose, mouse, viper, vixen, walrus, warthog

TIME TO RHYME 3

There are several suitable answers, including:
RED: bed, dread, fed, head, said
BLUE: chew, do, few, glue, who
GREEN: bean, clean, lean, mean, screen
WHITE: bite, fight, height, light, might
BLACK: hack, jack, pack, sack, track

THE BIG X WORD SEARCH 3

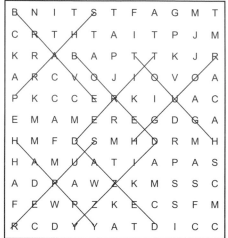

THE WORD STORE 3

There could be many answers, including:
Liz's teacher was amazed! Never before had her teacher seen such a piece of impressive writing. "This is great work," he told Liz. "You should think about becoming a novelist. You are extremely talented. Your parents will be delighted when they read this wonderful essay." Liz felt embarrassed. She hadn't realized she had ability; she just felt ordinary. But the comment from her teacher had made her feel more confident. "Who knows?" she thought. "Maybe one day I'll be famous!"

LETTERS 3

o	u	a	e	o	a	i	e	i	o
		i	a			o			u
		u	o			e			a
		a	e		o	a	i		u
						i			e
						e			o
		a	u			a			u
		u	o			u			i
		i	e			e			a
u	i	a	o	i	e	a	i	e	o

WORDS AND SOUNDS 3
"Don't ~~brake~~ / break your neck!" yelled Mom as Johnny rode / ~~road~~ down the ~~rode~~ / road quickly. "Avoid the ~~whole~~ / hole in the ground." "The ~~mane~~ / main street is okay," Johnny called back. "And anyway, I'm a ~~grate~~ / great cyclist!" Mom raised her eyebrows. "He'll wail / ~~whale~~ and ~~wine~~ / whine if he falls off." Last time he did that he was in ~~pane~~ / pain for days. / ~~daze~~. "Keep your feet on the pedals / ~~peddles~~!" she called after him.

SYNONYMS 3
Sleepy tired, false untrue, active lively, scared afraid, chilly icy, strange odd

ACRONYMS 3
There are many suitable answers, for example: MADS Mystery, Adventure and Dragon Society BKK Books for Kids in Kansas

DEFINITIONS 3
Gibbon 2) A large monkey
Globe 1) The planet earth
Millennium 3) One thousand years
Colossal 1) Huge
Intricate 2) Complicated

LEAPING LIZARD 3
Games and puzzles keep your mind sharp and supple

SYLLABLES 3
There are many suitable answers, for example:
Mop Money Monitor
Hand Handle Handkerchief
Bit Bigger Bicycle
Son Sorry Somebody

COMPOUND WORDS 3
Homework, mousetrap, birdbath, doorbell, trapdoor, bluebird, workshop, bathroom, butterfly

CONTINUOUS WORDS 3
Gold red green maroon brown indigo orange gray yellow white cream mauve purple scarlet violet turquoise blue silver lilac black lavender burgundy pink lime teal

SPEED WORDS 3
There are many suitable answers, for example:
1. THORN, 2. LATER, 3. CHEESE, 4. HAMMER, 5 ZONE

CONCENTRATION 3
The definite article has been underlined:
Wilma gets it right. Wilma smiled and got out her magic wand. Instantly, the boy's shoes came to life and Cody jumped up. He picked up the blue bucket, and ran wildly to the river. He staggered back with a heavy bucket of water. "Stop!" shouted Cody. "Someone stop these shoes!" "You are being silly," scolded his mom. "Shoes do not run on their own." Back and forth the shoes ran to the river with Cody inside them, struggling to carry the blue bucket, which seemed to get heavier each time. "I'm sorry,

I'm sorry!" he shouted to his mom. "I've learned my lesson. I'll be good for the rest of the day!" Mom raised her eyebrows. "Okay" she said, feeling bewildered. Wilma smiled, and the shoes stopped moving.

VOCABULARY 3
POWER PATTERN PUPPET PADDLE PEACH PANIC

CHANGE A LETTER 3
SAFE, SALT, MAKE, MAIL, TALL, HAIL, LAZY, LAKE, MAZE

HAT WORDS 3
There are many suitable answers, for example:
A, BY, CAT, DUCK, ELECT, FLIGHT, GORILLA, HEDGEHOG

CATEGORIES 3
MAMMAL: GIRAFFE, HARE, WOLF, KOALA
SEA CREATURE: STINGRAY, SQUID, EEL, LOBSTER
BIRD: THRUSH, SWALLOW, EAGLE, OWL

GRIDWORD 3

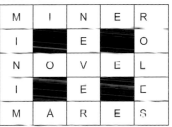

M	I	N	E	R
I		E		O
N	O	V	E	L
I		E		E
M	A	R	E	S

LIZARD IN A CAVE 3
The cave he would like to go in is underlined:
ARROW SWORD BLADE KNIFE <u>WHEEL</u>

HOW MANY 3
There are many suitable answers, for example:
1: BIT, CHILD, FISH, HID, KISS, LID, LIST, MILD, SHIP, TINY
2: HIDING, LIMIT
3: VISITING

CHANGE AND RHYME 3
There may be more than one solution
SCENT & WENT, NEWS & LOSE

Q CROSSWORDS 3
ACROSS. 1 SILLY, 4. PETAL
DOWN. 1. SLEEP, 2. YODEL, 3. STAMP

WHEEL WORDS 3
YELLOW, ORANGE, VIOLET, PURPLE, INDIGO

REMOVE A LETTER 3
I HAVE A NEW PET

AEIOU 3
FRESH, CORN, MARRY, PINE, NOUN

SKILLFUL SENTENCES 3
There are many suitable answers, for example:
"All boys can dance" explained Florence.
"George Hughes is jiving; Ken loves to mambo.
Nathan only plays quick rhythms so they
undertake Viennese Waltz. Xavier yearns
Zumba."

IN THE MIDDLE 3
Three Wise Men, Just in Time, Jack and Jill,
Bad Worse Worst, Peace on Earth, Rio de
Janeiro, President Barack Obama, Whole Half
Quarter.

WORD LINE 4

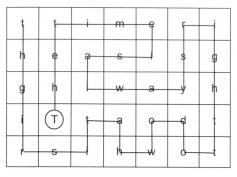

UMBRELLA WORDS 4
There are many suitable answers, for example:
ch: chap school watch
el: elephant steel yellow
pa: park plate spray
st: stamp sent faster

TRAIN WORDS 4
The words to find have been underlined: sh<u>oddy</u>,
so<u>oner</u>, wo<u>oden</u>, mo<u>ored</u>, me<u>owed</u>, sl<u>owly</u>

ANAGRAMS 4
Right wrong; soft hard; tall short; fat thin

ALPHABET TEASERS 4
There are many suitable answers, for example:

Begins with	Item in kitchen	Item in bathroom	Item in bedroom
S	Spoon	Soap	Sheet
B	Bowl	Bath	Blanket
T	Teaspoon	Toothbrush	Teddy bear
M	Microwave	Mirror	Mattress

FISHING 4
Red, ant, rat, near, dart, dear, tread

MINI WORD SUDOKU 4

d	g	i	r
r	i	d	g
g	d	r	i
i	r	g	d

ALPHABET 4
Tired, timid, silly, sickly, quiet, quaint, nosey,
noisy, happy, handsome, brave, brash

TIME TO RHYME 4
There are several suitable answers, including:
JAY: day, may, ray, stay, way
WREN: den, hen, men, pen, ten
LARK: bark, dark, park, shark, spark
GULL: cull, dull, hull, mull, skull
TERN: burn, churn, earn, fern, learn

THE BIG X WORD SEARCH 4

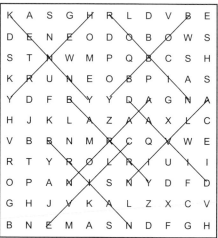

THE WORD STORE 4
There could be many answers, including:
"I can't find my calculator!" shouted Jack. "Can
I borrow somebody's phone instead?" Lily
looked at him. "Jack, you could lose anything,
even your head, if you aren't careful!" Jack
smiled. "Last week I lost my watch and my
jacket." "You're a dork," laughed Lily. "If I gave
you a meal you would probably drop it on the
floor!" "My brother wanted to give me a camera
for my birthday," said Jack, "but changed his
mind and gave me a book instead."

LETTERS 4

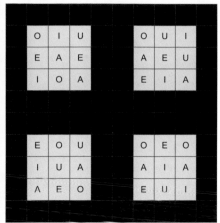

WORDS AND SOUNDS 4
BUCKLE

SYNONYMS 4
Allow permit, damage harm, knock hit, boast brag, change alter, repair mend

ACRONYMS 4
There are many suitable answers, for example:
VIPA Volleyball in Pennsylvania Association
KITS Kids in Tennis Society
WSS Water Sports Society

DEFINITIONS 4
Siesta 3) Afternoon nap
Wallaby 1) Small kangaroo
Oboe 2) Woodwind Instrument
Miracle 2) Extremely unusual and wonderful event
Radish 1) A vegetable

LEAPING LIZARD 4
Give yourself a compliment like your best friend would.

SYLLABLES 4
There are many suitable answers, for example:
Net Never Newspaper
Chat Chapel Charity
Stray Struggle Strawberry
Pot Police Politely

COMPOUND WORDS 4
There are many suitable answers, for example:
NEWS paper, reel, letter, clip, reader, stand, room, print, caster, boy
SEA gull, port, weed, sick, shell, scape, weed, shore, bird, side, board
SUN shine, dial, flower, bathe, day, baked, roof, down, glasses, lit

CONTINUOUS WORDS 4
Boots skirt trousers scarf shoes dress shirt suit tie vest belt blazer gloves shorts slacks blouse slippers socks pajamas sweater sneakers underpants sandals jeans jacket hat coat cardigan cap overalls

SPEED WORDS 4
There are many suitable answers, for example:
1. LEFT, 2. USUAL, 3. WIZARD, 4. MOTHER, 5. ELEPHANT

CONCENTRATION 4
The pronouns have been underlined:
Wilma and the wizard. The following week Wilma went to see Wilfred the Wizard. "Will you show me how to make a new potion?" she asked him. "Certainly," he replied. "Tell me what you want." "A potion to turn you and me into a prince and a princess," she said. They looked through the potion book together. He chose the best potion and they turned into a handsome prince and a beautiful princess. "Will you marry me?" he asked. "No," she replied. "Instead we will go on an adventure!"

VOCABULARY 4
ALLOWS ANYONE ARCHERY ARMPIT ARENA AWESOME

CHANGE A LETTER 4
BOSS, MASS, BATS, HARD, HARE, HARM, FIRE, CORE, FORK

HAT WORDS 4
There are many suitable answers, for example:
SO, SAY, SWIM, SHINE, SELECT, STATION, SLEEPING

CATEGORIES 4
ADJECTIVE: HONEST, EAGER, HAPPY
ADVERB: HONESTLY, EAGERLY, HAPPILY
NOUN: HONESTY, EAGERNESS, HAPPINESS

GRIDWORD 4

S	T	R	U	T
L		O		A
E	I	N	E	R
E		E		O
T	R	O	U	T

LIZARD IN A CAVE 4
The cave he would like to go in is underlined:
HELEN SUSAN JULIE JASON KAREN

HOW MANY 4
There are many suitable answers, for example:
1: DOG, FOLD, FROG, HOT, LOG, LORD, POD, POND, POT, STRONG
2: BOOK, FOLLOW, GOOD, ROBOT, ROOM, SOON
3: TOMORROW

CHANGE AND RHYME 4
There may be more than one solution
WHOLE & BOWL, RULE & FOOL

Q CROSSWORDS 4
ACROSS. 1. SCARF, 4. TEACH
DOWN. 1. START, 2. FRESH, 3. BACON

WHEEL WORDS 4
PARROT, PIGEON, CUCKOO, CANARY, THRUSH

REMOVE A LETTER 4
LET'S GO TO THE PARK

AEIOU 4
TWEET, ART, BUSH, TINT, SHOP

SKILLFUL SENTENCES 4
There are many suitable answers, for example: "He eats sausages," said Dad daily. "Yeah, he eats some," Ella agreed.

IN THE MIDDLE 4
Three Blind Mice, Over and Out, Yellow Brick Road, New York City, Morning Afternoon Evening, Caterpillar Chrysalis/Pupa Butterfly, Bacon Lettuce Tomato, Bird of Prey.

WORD LINE 5

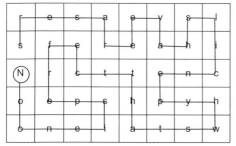

UMBRELLA WORDS 5
There are many suitable answers, for example:
ar: area cart later
gl: glove goal angle
ck: sock cake tickle
ry: ray railway very

TRAIN WORDS 5
The words to find have been underlined:
scribe, origin, triple, abides, Friday, crimes

ANAGRAMS 5
light dark; tight loose; clean dirty; rich poor

ALPHABET TEASERS 5
There are many suitable answers, for example:

Begins with	Relative	Insect	Fruit
G	Grandmother	Grasshopper	Grapefruit
B	Brother	Beetle	Banana
A	Aunt	Ant	Apple
M	Mother	Maggot	Mango

FISHING 5
Elf, has, seal, leaf, heal, flash, shelf

MINI WORD SUDOKU 5

a	z	m	e
e	m	z	a
m	e	a	z
z	a	e	m

ALPHABET 5
Beg, hip, gin, opt, art, fry, boy, lot, bow, den

TIME TO RHYME 5
There are several suitable answers, including:
OAK: croak, folk, joke, poke, spoke
ASH: bash, cash, lash, mash, rash
PINE: dine, line, mine, shine, wine
BEECH: each, leech, peach, reach, teach
CHERRY: berry, ferry, merry, sherry, very

THE BIG X WORD SEARCH 5

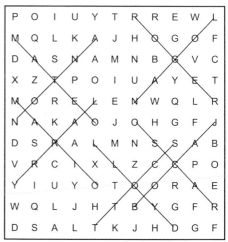

THE WORD STORE 5
There could be many answers, including:
"There are only bananas and sandwiches in the picnic basket," said Joy. "Has anyone got any cookies as well?" "I've got some apples and some grapes," said Phil. "Did someone bring juice?" asked Joy. "Let me go to the kitchen and see if we have any," said Jackie. She looked in the cupboard and even behind the microwave but couldn't find any. "I've found some water. Will that do?" she asked.
"Yes, great. Let's go," replied Joy.

LETTERS 5

g	t	r	h	t	u	d	z	w	u
k	f	c	y	w	r	c			k
p	t	f	o	z	p	o			g
f	o	w	y	d	e	w			u
c	h	e	d	u	k	t			z
y	z								f
k	y								h
e	g			c	z	e			p
w	u			k	h	o			u
c	t			p	t	h			y

WORDS AND SOUNDS 5
THUNDER

SYNONYMS 5
King ruler, rubbish trash, job occupation, writer author, sack bag, taxi cab

ACRONYMS 5
There are many suitable answers, for example:
ARK Art in Reno for Kids
YFM Young Film Makers
JAA Japanese Art and Animé

DEFINITIONS 5
Jackal 1) Wild animal
Braille 2) System of writing for people who are blind
Identical 1) The very same
Audible 3) Something you can hear
Smog 1) Heavy fog

LEAPING LIZARD 5
Fill your days with lots of fun and laughter

SYLLABLES 5
There are many suitable answers, for example:
Off Often Officer
Sell Sender Serious
Nap Nasty National
Ink Income Indigo

COMPOUND WORDS 5
There are many suitable answers, for example:
EYE brow, lid, ball, sight, lash, glasses, liner, brow, witness
SUPER man, natural, sonic, star, tanker, hero, human, market, structure
BLACK bird, smith, berry, board, jack, list, mail, ball, out

CONTINUOUS WORDS 5
Wolf lynx lion monkey wallaby bear zebra aardvark kangaroo ocelot tiger rhinoceros snake elephant anteater leopard alligator porcupine hyena armadillo ostrich chee-tah giraffe gazelle llama camel gorilla baboon panda badger beaver panther crocodile cougar bobcat jaguar puma

SPEED WORDS 5
There are many suitable answers, for example:
1. ATTACH, 2. SEVEN, 3. FLASK, 4. SACKS, 5. EDUCATION

CONCENTRATION 5
The adverbs have been underlined:
Arranging an adventure. Wilma and Wilfred thought carefully. "What kind of adventure should we go on?" asked Wilma the Princess excitedly. Cautiously Wilfred the Prince replied, "A quest to find the fire breathing dragon?" Wilma's eyes narrowed suspiciously.
"That will be dangerous…" A fire-breathing dragon wasn't what she had in mind for a handsome prince and a beautiful princess. "I know," Wilfred replied chirpily. "Dangerous but exciting!" "Okay . . ." said Wilma slowly, "but please figure out the arrangements quickly or else I may change my mind."

VOCABULARY 5
SHAMPOO SHUTTER SHADOW SHOPPING SHIMMER SHERRY

CHANGE A LETTER 5
RICH, RACE, MICE, LEEK, WEED, WEAK, SWAN, SWAP, SHAM

HAT WORDS 5
There are many suitable answers, for example:
MY, TRY, PLAY, CURRY, MELODY, TUESDAY, PHARMACY

CATEGORIES 5
ADJECTIVE: PERFECT, CORRECT, CERTAIN
ADVERB: PERFECTLY, CORRECTLY, CERTAINLY
NOUN: PERFECTION, CORRECTION, CERTAINTY

GRIDWORD 5

T	E	A	S	E
E		L		L
R	A	I	S	E
S		V		C
E	V	E	N	T

LIZARD IN A CAVE 5
The cave he would like to go in is underlined:
MARIA PETER JACOB DEREK BRIAN

HOW MANY 5
There are many suitable answers, for example:
1: BUD, BUSH, FUNNY, HUNT, HURRY, LUCK, NUT, PUT, TUB, TURN, SHUT, SUN
2: FUNGUS

CHANGE AND RHYME 5
There may be more than one solution
SHADE & MADE / STARE & MARE, BLUE & TOO

Q CROSSWORDS 5
ACROSS. 1. BUNNY, 4. STING
DOWN. 1. BOOTS, 2. YOUNG, 3. TIGER

WHEEL WORDS 5
KARATE, SKIING, TENNIS, HOCKEY, SOCCER

REMOVE A LETTER 5
I GOT IT AT THE MALL

AEIOU 5
MANY, TEST, LOW, POUR, SHIN

SKILLFUL SENTENCES 5
There are many suitable answers, for example:
Marie rode the blue bike. She came home alone.

IN THE MIDDLE 5
Three Legged Race, Out of Order, Wild Goose Chase, Frogspawn Tadpole Frog, Third Time Lucky, Up and Running, Salt Lake City, World War Two.

WORD LINE 6

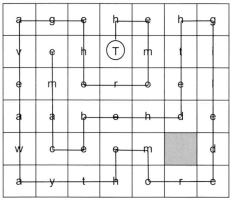

UMBRELLA WORDS 6
There are many suitable answers, for example:
qu: quick squash require
ma: made mean impact
in: into rain cushion
oa: oak float dollar

TRAIN WORDS 6
The words to find have been underlined: caters career derail defeat clears teased

ANAGRAMS 6
bacon eggs; salt pepper; fish chips; bread butter

ALPHABET TEASERS 6
There are many suitable answers, for example:

Begins with	Noun	Adjective	Verb
S	Ship	Silly	Sing
H	House	High	Help
M	Mouse	Muddy	Move
L	Lamp	Lucky	Laugh

FISHING 6
Cat, eat, the, chat, heat, cheat, teach

MINI WORD SUDOKU 6

a	l	**p**	n
n	p	l	a
p	n	a	**l**
l	**a**	n	p

ALPHABET 6
Ton, sea, rig, red, woe, lie, urn, spa, use, she

TIME TO RHYME 6
Wheat: beat, treat & heat
Bread: thread, tread & head
Phone: bone, tone & cone
Gnome: dome, tome & home
Go: yoyo, so & no

THE BIG X WORD SEARCH 6

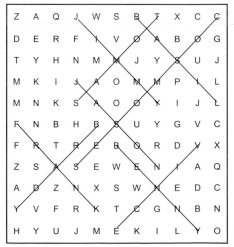

THE WORD STORE 6
There could be many answers, including: Mark looked at the big pile of books on the floor and thought, "How am I going to find my diary?" His friend had knocked them off the shelf when looking for his comic. He didn't find it, but did find a magazine and a poster that had been hidden for ages. "I'll buy a new one," thought Mark. On his way to the store he met Marie, his neighbor, who had a new phone AND a new tablet! Mark was surprised. Marie was OLD and old people didn't have those kinds of things! He expected her to buy things like hats and gloves.

LETTERS 6

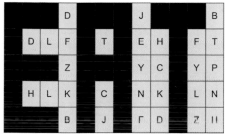

WORDS AND SOUNDS 6
There are many suitable answers, for example:
BAT: The bat flew down and landed on my baseball bat.
CAN: I can give you a can of lemonade.
BOW: I will bring my violin and bow and will put a bow in my hair.
COOL: The weather is cool in winter but I still look cool in my sunglasses.

SYNONYMS 6
Begin start, rip tear, brush sweep , smash shatter, see look, pull tug

ACRONYMS 6
There are many suitable answers, for example:
SAS Superheroes and Superheroines
MR Manga Readers
YAC Youth Adventure Comics

DEFINITIONS 6
Kimono 3) Japanese robe
Hygiene 2) Keeping clean and healthy
Quiff 1) Curl of hair on forehead
Lyre 2) Instrument like a harp
Hostile 1) Unfriendly

LEAPING LIZARD 6
Did you know that word puzzles help with spelling?

SYLLABLES 6
There are many suitable answers, for example:
Arm Arrow Artistic
Eat Early Eagerly
Bell Better Beginning
Chest Cheetah Cheeseburger

COMPOUND WORDS 6
There are many suitable answers, for example:
FIRE works, fly, fighter, cracker, ball, man, proof, arms, break
BACK bone, log, pack, hand, track, stroke, stage, fire, drop, ache
SOME one, what, where, thing, how, body, day, place

CONTINUOUS WORDS 6
Judge coach nurse editor professor doctor pilot poet teacher barber baker broker actor farmer mechanic chauffeur chef firefighter pharmacist dentist tailor soldier printer waiter watchmaker athlete accountant vet-erinarian beautician banker actress salesman magician musician author sailor policeman politician carpenter engineer fisherman craftsman waitress butcher shoemaker lawyer

SPEED WORDS 6
There are many suitable answers, for example:
1. HIP, 2. GOING, 3. MOUSE, 4. SIXTY, 5. TOOT

CONCENTRATION 6
The comparatives and superlatives have been underlined:
Wilma and Wilfred on an adventure. It wasn't the best trip that Wilma had ever been on. Climbing the rocky mountains was harder than she expected, and crossing shark-infested rivers was definitely the worst part. "Meeting a fire-breathing dragon will be easier than this," she grumbled as she waded through the river, her princess dress getting wetter and messier. Wilfred, however, was fooling more excited with each step he took. "We're getting nearer to the dragon!" he shouted excitedly. "I can see the biggest dragon flames I've ever seen!" Wilma sighed. This wasn't the princess-type of adventure she had hoped for.

VOCABULARY 6
HELMET HARMONY HASSLE HONEST HEARTH HAMPER

CHANGE A LETTER 6
NOTE, ROSE, NOSY, EVEN, OPEN, OVER, GATE, DARE, DATA

HAT WORDS 6
There are many suitable answers, for example:
ME, THE, TIME, VERSE, MINUTE, CLIMATE, NICKNAME

CATEGORIES 6
PEOPLE: HUMOROUS, CHARMING, CONFIDENT, CREATIVE, SUCCESSFUL
ANIMALS: TAME, SCALY, POISONOUS, FEROCIOUS, PLAYFUL

GRIDWORD 6

C	O	L	I	C
O	■	I	■	A
M	I	N	I	M
I	■	E	■	E
C	A	R	O	L

LIZARD IN A CAVE 6
The cave he would like to go in is underlined:
HIPPO RHINO WHALE MOUSE ZEBRA

HOW MANY 6
There are many suitable answers, for example:
1: BLESS, BOSS, CHESS, DRESS, FUSS,
HAPPINESS, HISS, MASS, MISSED, PASS,
SENSE, SPLASH
2: CLASSES

CHANGE AND RHYME 6
There may be more than one solution
LOAD & ROAD, HERB & VERB

Q CROSSWORDS 6
ACROSS. 1. WHITE, 4. ERROR
DOWN. 1. WHALE, 2. ENTER, 3. DRINK

WHEEL WORDS 6
MUSEUM, PALACE, GARAGE, CHURCH,
PRISON

REMOVE A LETTER 6
FOUR PLUS FOUR IS EIGHT

AEIOU 6
WIFE, BAKE, SOAK, FLUNG, SHELL

SKILLFUL SENTENCES 6
There are many suitable answers, for example:
Many pupils stood around.
"What's going on?" Joy said.
"Nothing," said Mr. Brown. "Go back to your
classrooms."

WORD LINE 7

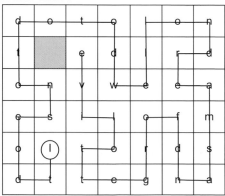

UMBRELLA WORDS 7
There are many suitable answers, for example
we: west tower write
bi: bin brain orbit
ff: coffee stuff fulfill
th: then trash with

TRAIN WORDS 7
The words to find have been underlined:
rapyaa, arbyap, ybarpa, prbayp, yabray,
apayrb

ANAGRAMS 7
cup saucer; pots pans; shoes socks; soap
water

ALPHABET TEASERS 7
There are many suitable answers, for example:

Begins with	Noun	Adjective	Verb
D	Duck	Dry	Dance
V	Vest	Vast	Vanish
J	Jug	Jolly	Jump
T	Toe	Tiny	Twist

FISHING 7
Son, ice, coin, once, nice, since, noise

MINI WORD SUDOKU 7

a	b	n	y	r	i
i	r	y	n	b	a
r	y	i	a	n	b
b	n	a	i	y	r
n	i	b	r	a	y
y	a	r	b	i	n

ALPHABET 7
Milk, glee, jail, deaf, hall, able, made, lime,
break, chef

TIME TO RHYME 7
Flour: sour & hour
Mower: blower, rower, & lower
Toll: scroll, stroll & roll
Grace: lace, face & race
Spear: hear, dear & near

THE BIG X WORD SEARCH 7

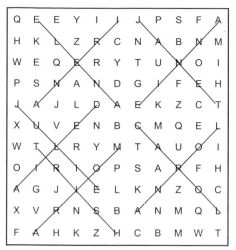

THE WORD STORE 7
There could be many answers, including:
Eddie liked to sing while his sister Dora liked to dance. Sometimes they would practice together. "Please don't bother your mother today," said Dad. "Just go outside and play." Eddie and Dora giggled. Dora looked at Eddie and smiled. Eddie looked at Dora and said, "Let's annoy Mom and Dad!" So they jumped and ran and laughed, but they didn't want to shout in case they got in trouble.

LETTERS 7

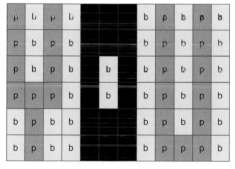

WORDS AND SOUNDS 7
There are many suitable answers, for example:
DEAR: It's too dear, even for a dear friend of mine.
KIND: What kind of person is he? A kind, generous one.
PARK: Mom is going to park by the park.
ROCK: The rock star sat on a rock.

SYNONYMS 7
Peaceful calm, rough coarse, rich wealthy, unusual peculiar, perfect faultless, pleasant enjoyable

ACRONYMS 7
There are many suitable answers, for example:
DIG Digital Interest Group
PAM Phones and More
CoCoC Connecticut Computer Club

DEFINITIONS 7
Umpteen 1) A lot
Consequence 3) What happens as a result
Quaint 2) Dainty, old fashioned
Jovial 3) Merry, good humored
Nettle 1) Stinging plant

LEAPING LIZARD 7
You can learn a lot when using a dictionary.

SYLLABLES 7
There are many suitable answers, for example:
Tent Tennis Terrible
Word Woman Wonderful
Hip Hilly History
Not Noble Normally

COMPOUND WORDS 7
There are many suitable answers, for example:
Mean, day, night, air, tea, bed, meal, summer, winter, life TIME
Hand, school, mail, wind, flea, bean, gas, sand, money, saddle BAG
Green, out, dog, farm, town, tree, hot, jail, ware, bird HOUSE

CONTINUOUS WORDS 7
Ship wish dish shed shift fish push shut blush shrub cash clash share rash harsh fresh marsh shame sheep shop show posh brush bush

SPEED WORDS 7
There are many suitable answers, for example:
1. METER, 2. DRY, 3. CURRY, 4. QUARTER, 5. PILLOW

CONCENTRATION 7
1. 13, 2. 25

VOCABULARY 7
DRAMATIC DRAGON DRUMMER DRAWER DRIBBLE DRAPES DRANK

CHANGE A LETTER 7
DAMP, DOME, DOOR, SOUR, CARS, EARN, EAST, VASE, DUTY, DULL

HAT WORDS 7
There are many suitable answers, for example:
WE, WHY, WEST, WHEAT, WIZARD, WEATHER, WINDMILL

CATEGORIES 7
SOUTH AMERICA: ARGENTINA, BRAZIL, PERU
EUROPE: SPAIN, FRANCE, GERMANY
AFRICA: UGANDA, NIGERIA, KENYA

GRIDWORD 7

LIZARD IN A CAVE 7
The cave he would like to go in is underlined:
BERRY <u>ONION</u> PEACH MANGO GRAPE

HOW MANY 7
There are many suitable answers, for example:
1: BALL, CHILL, DOLL, FULL, GULL, HOLLY, LEVEL, LIKELY, LILAC, LILY, PULL, WELL
2: LOLLIPOP

CHANGE AND RHYME 7
There may be more than one solution
TOUCH & MUCH, FOUR & CORE

Q CROSSWORDS 7
ACROSS. 1. SUGAR, 4. GREEN
DOWN. 1. SWING, 2. ROBIN, 3. SEVEN

WHEEL WORDS 7
MIRROR, SHOWER, CARPET, TEAPOT, BUCKET

REMOVE A LETTER 7
THE SUN IS SETTING

AEIOU 7
CANDLE, WENT, SOUR, FISH, COOL

SKILLFUL SENTENCES 7
There are many suitable answers, for example:
"Aha!" Bob said to Anna. "At noon we'll get a kayak and a racecar."

WORD LINE 8

	r	e	t	t	a	m		t	c	(N)
h			i	s	e	o	o		a	o
o			e	v		m		f	k	i
w	a	s	d	e	s	s	e			n
s	m	a	w					n	d	

UMBRELLA WORDS 8
There are many suitable answers, for example:
ve: vest give vote
ai: aim remain alive
on: once moon hoping
ze: zebra maze ozone

TRAIN WORDS 8
The words to find have been underlined: gllale, elagea, algele, gleage, lelega, gallel

ANAGRAMS 8
pen paper; hammer nail; knife fork; lock key

ALPHABET TEASERS 8
There are many suitable answers, for example:

Begins with	Noun	Adjective	Verb
I	Ice	Interesting	Ignore
K	Kite	Keen	Kick
W	Witch	Wicked	Wait
Y	Yoyo	Young	Yell

FISHING 8
Sew, rip, sip, wire, wise, spire, swipe

MINI WORD SUKOKU 8

l	a	i	n	g	s
g	s	n	l	i	a
n	g	l	s	a	i
s	i	a	g	l	n
i	n	g	a	s	l
a	l	s	i	n	g

ALPHABET 8
Story, torn, pour, worst, rusty, trout, swoop, potty, worry, nouns

TIME TO RHYME 8
Foe: woe, toe & hoe
Sincere: severe, sphere & here
Enough: tough & rough
Mature: sure, cure & pure
Relies: dries, ties & pies

THE BIG X WORD SEARCH 8

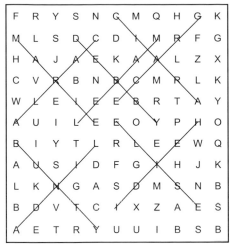

THE WORD STORE 8
There could be many answers, including:
Kira stared at the box. "Yes, please open it," she said, "but don't damage it." Jordan questioned her. "Are you sure? I can hold it and carry it if you'd like me to?" Kira tutted. "No, don't touch. It may break if you do that." Jordan wanted to squeeze it. "Stop!" Kira yelled. "Put it down!"

LETTERS 8

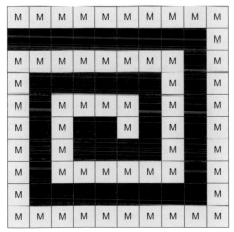

WORDS AND SOUNDS 8
There are many suitable answers, for example:
ROW: Don't row the boat past that row of yachts.
TIE: I'll use my school tie to tie up the broken fence.
TRIP: I saw her trip when we were on the school trip.
WAVE: I'll wave to the boat when it reaches the top of the wave.
WATCH: Please watch your items or someone may steal your watch.

SYNONYMS 8
Ugly unattractive, honest truthful, unpleasant nasty, clever wise, upset distressed, last final

ACRONYMS 8
There are many suitable answers, for example:
BUG Boston Uniform Group
CoRP Costumes for Role Play
CCC Creators of Cool Costumes

DEFINITIONS 8
Armadillo 3) An animal with a hard back
Kilt 2) Skirt made of tartan cloth
Erase 1) Rub out, delete
Treble 2) Three times as many
Yodel 3) Singing of Swiss mountain dwellers

LEAPING LIZARD 8
Grandparents and grandchildren together get up to no good!

SYLLABLES 8
There are many suitable answers, for example:
Sly Slipper Sleepily
Top Tonic Tomato
Like Lively Limited
Press Printer President

COMPOUND WORDS 8
There are many suitable answers, for example:
Candle, flood, day, night, search, lime, star, sky, head LIGHT
Match, broom, drum, chop, dip, joy, lip, yard, fiddle, slap STICK
Mail, gear, cash, lunch, boom, post, hat, shoe, tool, juke BOX

CONTINUOUS WORDS 8
Pizza zap puzzle zero zoom maze zone nuzzle zebra dazzle daze quiz zany haze whizz zing grizzle buzzard quartz jazz waltz laze

SPEED WORDS 8
There are many suitable answers, for example:
1. DOLL, 2. LOOSE, 3. MAGIC, 4. ABOUT, 5. FORT

CONCENTRATION 8
1. 8, 2. 5

VOCABULARY 8
WRAPPED WAGON WADDLE WHIMPER WRIGGLE WEEKLY WRANGLE

CHANGE A LETTER 8
STEM, SEEK, SNOW, SHOE, DUET, SUIT, ROAD, REAR, PATE, BATH

HAT WORDS 8
There are many suitable answers, for example:
GO, LOT, POND, FORCE, POWDER, ROMANCE, MOONBEAM

CATEGORIES 8
AMERICAN: AX, ARMOR, COLOR, GRAY, METER, BEHAVIOR
BRITISH: AXE, ARMOUR, COLOUR, GREY, METRE, BEHAVIOUR

GRIDWORDS 8

LIZARD IN A CAVE 8
The cave he would like to go in is underlined:
VIDEO MUSIC RADIO PIANO <u>COMIC</u> FLUTE

HOW MANY 8
There are many suitable answers, for example
1: BATTLE, BOTTLE, GROTTO, PRETTY, SETTLE, SHUTTLE, STATE, TENT, THAT, TREAT, TOAST, TURTLE
2: STUTTER

CHANGE AND RHYME 8
There may be more than one solution
SEW & BLOW, SOUR & TOWER

Q CROSSWORDS 8
ACROSS. 1. HELLO, 4. HUMAN
DOWN. 1. HUTCH, 2. OFTEN, 3. SMALL

WHEEL WORDS 8
DOCTOR, POLICE, BARBER, ARTIST, JOCKEY, EDITOR

REMOVE A LETTER 8
THE STARS SHINE AT NIGHT

AEIOU 8
BUNCH , BLESS, CLASS, FRILL, COST

SKILLFUL SENTENCES 8
There are many suitable answers, for example:
"I'll eat the meat," said Pete, "then meet and greet people in the street and give them a treat."

WORD LINE 9

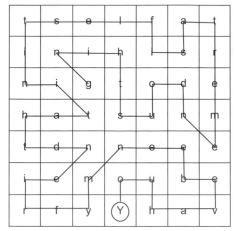

UMBRELLA WORDS 9
There are many suitable answers, for example:
ex: expand flex appendix
ty: type pretty tiny
id: idea paid rained
lc: local lilac volcano

TRAIN WORDS 9
The words to find have been underlined: ra<u>idil</u>, dar<u>lid</u>, a<u>iri</u>al, ali<u>ail</u>, d<u>all</u>ri, dri<u>ll</u>d

ANAGRAMS 9
read write; rise fall; stars stripes; lost found

ALPHABET TEASERS 9
There are many suitable answers, for example:

Begins with	Noun	Adjective	Verb
TH	Thumb	Thick	Think
TR	Trap	Tricky	Try
CH	Church	Chilly	Choose
CR	Crown	Crusty	Cry

FISHING 9
Raw, new, rent, wren, wart, tear, water

MINI WORD SUDOKU 9

i	n	u	t	m	e
t	m	e	n	i	u
m	t	n	u	e	i
u	e	i	m	n	t
e	u	m	i	t	n
n	i	t	e	u	m

ALPHABET 9

"Calm down, you look like you've seen a ghost!" said Jordan's dad. "I think I have—inside that open closet!" replied Jordan. "No, it wouldn't be able to get in. It's full of tunics," smiled Dad.

TIME TO RHYME 9

Leak: weak, streak & beak
Show: grow, know & snow
Ajar: afar, car & star
Mini: taxi, broccoli & ski
Ghost: post, host & most

THE BIG X WORD SEARCH 9

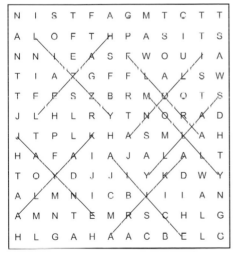

THE WORD STORE 9

There could be many answers, including:
Rachel loved to make cupcakes. Everybody said they were tasty. even delicious She would make them every week and sell them at the market. However, what people didn't realize was that the cupcakes were made from special ingredients, magical things like butterfly tails, a jar of raindrops, and a fairy's smile. She would stir them together with a magical spoon made from enchanted silver. Watching people eat her magical cupcakes made Rachel very happy.

WORDS AND SOUNDS 9

There are many suitable answers, for example:
H: Harry helped Henry's hungry hedgehog.
L: Laura likes Lily's little lamb.
A: Armadillos are always awesome.
B: Bella borrowed Bruno's books.
N: Nan never noticed Norma's new necklace.

SYNONYMS 9

Kidnap capture, lose misplace, stop cease, gather collect, reply answer, rest relax

ACRONYMS 9

There are many suitable answers, for example:
MCC Mountain Climbing for Children
YoDA Young Daring Adventurers
OBI Orienteering for Beginners Inc.

DEFINITIONS 9

Omega 2) Last letter of Greek alphabet
Famished 2) Extremely hungry
Summit 1) The top
Urban 3) Living in a city
Heron 2) Long-legged bird

LEAPING LIZARD 9

It's good to eat well and do lots of exercise.

SYLLABLES 9

There are many suitable answers, for example:
Stack Stagger Stadium
Boot Bookshelf Boomerang
Yet Yellow Yesterday
Zoo Zero Zodiac

COMPOUND WORDS 9

There are many suitable answers, for example:
Basket, volley, beach, curve, snow, cannon, base, foot, eye, gum BALL
Bill, clip, hard, key, dart, score, side, skate, head, story, over BOARD
Try, with, burn, shoot, stake, black, white, look, hide, knock OUT

CONTINUOUS WORDS 9

Sweet west stew weather when new went towel tower weep power web brew answer weed dwell lower week twelve tweet vowel twenty flower were few

SPEED WORDS 9

There are many suitable answers, for example:
1. FINGER, 2. KNOCK, 3. PARK, 4. DRAGON, 5. FOGGY

CONCENTRATION 9

1. 9, 2. 13

VOCABULARY 9

ALRIGHT WHISPER CAPTURE PLAYER HEATER ASTRIDE SMELLY

CHANGE A LETTER 9

LIMB, WARM, BURY, FULL, CASH, TOOL, WREN, SNAP, WARS, WAIT

HAT WORDS 9

There are many suitable answers, for example:
AT, STY, STOP, STRAY, STREET, STRANGE, STAR-FISH

CATEGORIES 9

AMERICAN: CENTER, TIRES, LABOR, REALIZE, PAJAMAS, PROGRAM
BRITISH: CENTRE, TYRES, LABOUR, REALISE, PYJAMAS, PROGRAMME

GRIDWORD 9

	S		A		S
C	L	O	S	E	T
	E		C		R
	E		E		E
S	P	O	N	G	E
	S		T		T

LIZARD IN A CAVE 9

The cave he would like to go in is underlined:
BREAD PASTA <u>JUICE</u> TOAST JELLY CHIPS

HOW MANY 9

There are many suitable answers, for example
1: APPLE, GRIPPED, HAPPY, PAPER, PEEP, PEOPLE, POPCORN, PREPARE, PURPLE, WRAPPER
2: PEPPER, POPPY

CHANGE AND RHYME 9

There may be more than one solution
SIGN & MINE, ANT & PANT

Q CROSSWORDS 9

ACROSS. 1. HORSE, 4. LUNCH
DOWN. 1. HOTEL, 2. EARTH, 3. UNDER

WHEEL WORDS 9

WICKED, NARROW, HUNGRY, BRAINY, FLUFFY, TENDER

REMOVE A LETTER 9

HE BOUGHT PEN AND PAPER

AEIOU 9

GLOVE, STEP, CLUB, GRAB, SPOIL

SKILLFUL SENTENCES 9

There are many suitable answers, for example:
"Silly Billy!" called Poppy cheerfully.

WORD LINE 10

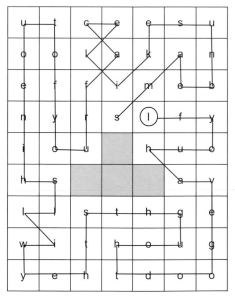

UMBRELLA WORDS 10

There are many suitable answers, for example:
je: jelly juice object
pu: push input sprout
dw: dwelling draw sandwich
eo: people fellow geography

TRAIN WORDS 10

The words to find have been underlined: te<u>sett</u>, be<u>seet</u>, <u>tebbes</u>, <u>bee</u>ste, ste<u>bet</u>, <u>steest</u>

ANAGRAMS 10
give take; flesh blood; bride groom; sooner later

ALPHABET TEASERS 10
There are many suitable answers, for example:

Begins with	Noun	Adjective	Verb
SW	Swing	Sweet	Sweep
FR	Frog	Frozen	Fry
PL	Plant	Pleasant	Play
QU	Quilt	Quiet	Quack

FISHING 10
Ask, cash, sack, shack, chalk, slack, clash

MINI WORD SUDOKU 10

a	c	o	t	i	n
t	n	i	c	o	a
i	a	t	o	n	c
c	o	n	i	a	t
n	i	c	a	t	o
o	t	a	n	c	i

ALPHABET 10
"Qui<u>ckly</u>—go le<u>ft</u>, and we'll make it to the Ro<u>xy</u> cinema in time!"
"What's <u>th</u>is movie ab<u>ou</u>t?"
"<u>Om</u>nivore tig<u>ers</u>."
"<u>S</u>erio<u>u</u>sly, dude?"
"Well, <u>not</u> ju<u>st</u> that…"

TIME TO RHYME 10
Flea: tea, sea & pea
Device: price, mice & rice
Nose: pose, hose & rose
Revise: advise, rise & wise
Enable: stable, disable & table

THE BIG X WORD SEARCH 10

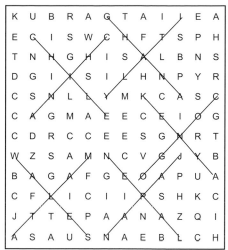

THE WORD STORE 10
There could be many answers, including:
Every time Tom walked past the gallery he saw some beautiful paintings in there. He didn't buy any but he did admire them. One day there was a terrible storm that damaged everything in the town. Everything, that is, except the things in the gallery that Tom walked past. "How odd," he thought. "Have some special forces been at play?" He decided to investigate. All kinds of things were in there; unusual things like blankets made from feathers and carpets made from lavender.

LETTERS 10

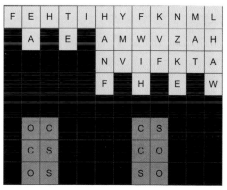

WORDS AND SOUNDS 10
There are many suitable answers, for example:
T: Toni's ten treacle tarts tasted terrific.
C: Can Catherine cut Carlo's cake?
S: Sally sent Simon some stamps.
E: Everyone escaped except Emma.
PH: Philip phoned Phoenix Pharmacy.

SYNONYMS 10
Leader chief, nuisance bother, rascal rogue, bucket pail, infant baby, beam ray

ACRONYMS 10
There are many suitable answers, for example:
DWL Dog Walkers League
POPS Phoenix Older Person's Supporters
CoUGH Community of Utah Garden Helpers

DEFINITIONS 10
Typhoon 3) A hurricane
Phobia 1) A strong fear
Tigon 2) A creature born from a tiger and lioness
Thistle 1) A prickly plant
Naïve 3) Innocent

LEAPING LIZARD 10
Children have one type of silliness and grown-ups have another.

SYLLABLES 10
There are many suitable answers, for example:
Then Therefore Theater
Sold Soldier Solution
Wind Winner Willingly
Lamp Ladder Landlady

COMPOUND WORDS 10
Fortnight, butterfly, earthworm, ballroom, sunbathe, starfish, hamburger, honeymoon, passport

CONTINUOUS WORDS 10
Below bless blue bubble bell noble blood dabble blend belt tremble blade bland humble blame bald able belong oblong blog blow bowl blank balance bleach rumble bull

SPEED WORDS 10
There are many suitable answers, for example:
1. ERASE, 2. VIOLET, 3. MOMENT, 4. IGLOO, 5. SCHOOL

CONCENTRATION 10
Which 2, Witch 7, Where 8, Were 6

VOCABULARY 10
POORLY COFFEE PLEASURE CLOTHES BELIEVE THOUGHT BENEATH GLOBE

CHANGE A LETTER 10
ACRE, BARN, DRUM, OILY, HUNT, OINK, SWAY, ITEM, OOZE, UNIT

HAT WORDS 10
There are many suitable answers, for example:
OX, BOX, EXIT, EXTRA, EXPECT, EXPLODE, EXERCISE

CATEGORIES 10
JAPANESE: SUSHI, JUDO, KARAOKE, SUMO
ITALIAN: PIZZA, LASAGNE, RISOTTO, PASTA
FRENCH: TABLE, GRAND, VOYAGE, PARDON

GRIDWORD 10

	K		S		C
T	A	T	T	O	O
	R		O		F
	A		A		F
S	T	A	T	U	E
	E		S		E

LIZARD IN A CAVE 10
The cave he would like to go in is underlined:
GOOSE LLAMA HYENA CAMEL <u>GECKO</u> OTTER

HOW MANY 10
There are many suitable answers, for example:
1: BABY, BARBER, BOMB, BULB, CABBAGE, HOBBY, PEBBLE, RABBIT, RIBBON, SUBURB
2: BOBBLE, BUBBLE

CHANGE AND RHYME 10
There may be more than one solution
SAID & BED, PLAY & THEY

Q CROSSWORDS 10
ACROSS. 1. PEACH, 4. ANGRY
DOWN. 1. PIZZA, 2. HAPPY, 3. AGENT

WHEEL WORDS 10
CEREAL, WALNUT, CHEESE, SALAMI, BURGER, MUESLI

REMOVE A LETTER 10
I OFTEN READ MANY BOOKS

AEIOU 10
CURRY, FINE, MARSH, ROW, BELT

SKILLFUL SENTENCES 10
There are many suitable answers, for example:
"Emma, I'd like a big black bag," called Jackie.

ANSWERS TO BONUS PUZZLES

ADJECTIVES AND NOUNS 1
There are many suitable answers, for example:
MASSIVE MOUSE; CURIOUS CRABS;
BROWN BACON; BAD BREAD; RED ROAD;
FAST FEET.

VOWEL SWAP 1
BLANKET, CARPET, MOTHER, PICKED,
PILLOW, SOFA, TABLE, TIME
"It's time for bed," said my mother, so I got
off the sofa, picked my books off the carpet,
and put them on the table. After going to the
bathroom, I snuggled under the blanket, my
head on the soft pillow.

NUMBER WORDS 1
There are many suitable answers, for example:
AM, AT, BE, IN, IS
OFF, OLD, OWL, OWN, OUT
BONE, CONE, DONE, GONE, STONE